Knife Fight!

Stringer grabbed the girl's elbow with his left hand and charged first, the knife blade in his right fist coming up low and dirty to rip the big man's guts from groin to breastbone . . .

The bully of the bunch could see that he meant it as he leaped backwards with a chicken squawk to land a good six feet back. Another gang member made a hesitant move toward Stringer from his right, and Stringer slashed his shirt and some belly fat before he too crawfished back through a picket fence bleating, *"Hijo de puerca! You cut me!"*

"My mistake," Stringer snapped. "I was out to kill you."

LOU CAMERON

STRINGER

AND THE DEADLY FLOOD

CHARTER BOOKS, NEW YORK

STRINGER AND THE DEADLY FLOOD

A Charter Book / published by arrangement with
the author

PRINTING HISTORY
Charter edition / September 1988

ISBN: 1-55773-070-9

Charter Books are published by The Berkley Publishing Group,
200 Madison Avenue, New York, N.Y. 10016.
The name "CHARTER" and the "C" logo are trademarks belonging
to Charter Communications Inc.

PRINTED IN THE UNITED STATES OF AMERICA

10 9 8 7 6 5 4 3 2 1

STRINGER

AND THE DEADLY FLOOD

CHAPTER
ONE

Earth tremors went with the fog and fleas of Frisco and seldom caused as much embarrassment as the one Stringer was suffering as he crept down the boarding-house stairs by the dawn's early light. He'd had to resort to sneaking to work in the mornings ever since the gal on the second landing had taken to leaving her door invitingly open. She worked odd hours as a nude model over on Russian Hill, and if she owned any clothing at all Stringer had yet to notice. Besides, it was mighty distracting at any hour to pass an open doorway with a naked lady on the bed inside blowing violet-scented tobacco smoke and sending knowing looks his way while he had to pass as best he could.

But this particular morning, to Stringer's relief, her door was barely ajar when he got down to her landing. He could hear her purring or snoring in there. He started to ease by softly—or tried to anyways, for just about then the city of San Francisco readjusted her corset with a mighty heave and the next thing Stringer knew he'd crashed into the room to join the gal on her bed.

She awoke to find the fully dressed Stringer across her naked lap. Sitting bolt upright, she regarded the seat of his pants with some confusion before she asked him, "I give up. Do you want me to spank you or is this a novel way of introducing yourself, Mister MacKail?"

He sprang off her and the bed, ears burning. "I suspect we just had an earthquake, ma'am."

She shrugged her bare shoulders, "Oh, I had hoped you were just being impetuous." Then she yawned and eyed him with renewed interest. "But as long as you're here, would you mind closing the hall door before you leap on me again? I don't think our landlady shares our, ah, Bohemian views on boarding house manners."

Stringer didn't, either. Not because he was a prude, but because a gent who messed with gals where he boarded had to be at least as dumb as a gent who messed with the gals where he drew his paycheck. So he shot her a gallantly regretful smile and told her, "I got to get to work now, no offense."

She lay back down, fully and invitingly exposed, shut her eyes again, and sighed. "My mother warned me the men I'd meet in this big, wicked city would treat me just awful. I had no idea how right her warning would turn out to be."

Stringer agreed life in the big city could be pure hell, then got out of there before his resolve could weaken. He had to walk a full block down the slopes of Rincon Hill before his damn-fool erection calmed down enough for comfortable walking in his too-tight city pants. He hated wearing a suit to work instead of the more comfortable cowhand duds he'd been raised in. But downtown Frisco was inclined to sneer at gents dressed cow. And judging from some of the superior looks he got that morning, it didn't approve much more of a gent duded up in a soft collar and an inexpensive suit. To look at the snappy Bay Area gents on their way to work, no one would suspect the businessmen running things of late were the near-descendants of the ragged-ass '49ers and the gussied up gals who'd followed them out west to get rich.

Impervious to any stares directed his way that early morning, Stringer crossed Market Street and headed up Montgomery to the cast-iron classic front of the *San Francisco Sun*. He almost tripped over a brace of stenographers as the three of them tried to enter at the same time. One of them was at least as pretty as the gal on the second landing, and he made an effort not to picture her with her hair down and that Gibson Girl middy blouse out of the way. It wasn't easy, but a man did what a man just had to do. So he wasn't thinking dirty when he entered the frosted-glass cubicle where they kept Sam Barca, their feature editor, out of harm or temptation's way.

The crusty old editor never invited anyone to have a seat, so Stringer just hauled in a handy bentwood chair and plunked it down next to old Sam's cluttered desk. As he sat astride it, resting his elbows on the back of the chair, he said, "Morning, boss. Where were you when that earthquake hit this morning?"

Barca growled, "Right here, of course. Unlike some lazy free-lance stringers I could mention, they expect me to punch that goddamned time clock out front. Besides, it wasn't much of a jolt, and even if it had been we wouldn't be running it. It's against the editorial policy of this paper to even intimate that the Golden State is subject to occasional rain or, God forbid, wobbly underpinnings." Barca rummaged through the clutter on his desk. "I've vouchered that feature you did on Bully Teddy's Great White Fleet, though I had to blue-pencil a lot of your smart-ass remarks to make the piece presentable. So what are you working on now?"

"I'm stuck for a new angle on whitewashed battleships," Stringer replied. Then he asked thoughtfully, "Did you know they built the main water reservoir of this town smack on an earthquake fault, Sam?"

Barca shrugged. "They had to build it some damned place, and I just told you we don't run earth tremor stories in the *Sun*, damn it."

Stringer reached inside his city vest for the cowboy makings he preferred to smoke, insisting, "One of these days we're going to have to. In their infinite wisdom the city engineers laid all the water mains our fire department may ever need right across some other known faults. When, not if, we ever get a real earthquake, every fire hydrant in town figures to go out of business about the same time."

"We're not paid to find faults in or about this fair city, damn it," Sam Barca snapped. "Half our classified ads deal with real estate. How do you feel about doing another exposé of the goddamned *Octopus*, MacKail?"

Stringer frowned thoughtfully down at the smoke he was rolling. "I dunno, Sam. Beating up on the Southern Pacific Railroad strikes me as a mite old hat since Frank Norris wrote that book-length exposé at the turn of the century and called it the Octopus. Made old C. P. Huntington so mad he died, they say. But I hear his nephew and only heir, Henry Huntington, has been running the family railroad pretty decent of late."

Barca glowered with genuine distaste. "Toad squat! Creep Huntington may be dead, but the apple never falls far from the tree and the whole damned family should have been hung for murder years ago!"

As Stringer sealed his cigarette with a lick of his tongue and put it between his lips, Barca droned on, "I was about your age when I covered the Massacre at Mussel Slough for this very paper. To drum up business for his railroad, Creep Huntington lured settlers into the arid wastes of Tulare County with promises to sell 'em railroad grant land at two or three dollars an acre. Then, once he had the poor suckers there, he upped the price to fifteen to forty bucks an acre instead."

Stringer ventured cautiously, "Nobody ever accused C. P. Huntington of being less than a hard-headed businessman, Sam. But, like I said, the man is dead."

Barca ignored his younger visitor's interruption as he cut back in. "So are a number of other gents, all murdered by the Southern Pacific in the Year of Our Lord 1880. When Creep Huntington sent railroad dicks under a tame U.S. marshal to evict the settlers who just couldn't pay his jacked-up prices, the battle that ensued took the lives of seven men. Most of them were settlers, and of course even the survivors had to pay up or get out in the end. I reported it when it happened, twenty years before Frank Norris got it in print. Naturally, nobody was willing to run such a story while Creep Huntington and his private army of hired guns were still holding full sway. I was mad as hell. Like I said, I was about your age then. It takes a man a while to learn he's just not big enough to change the world with his writings. The asshole who said the pen was mightier than the sword must have never worked for a publication that runs railroad advertising."

Stringer blew a lazy smoke ring before he nodded. "Well, if you need a rehash of the Battle of Mussel Slough I reckon I can go through the morgue and see if I can come up with a new angle."

Barca shook his head. "News that's old enough to vote is hardly news. We may have more recent crimes to pin on the Southern Pacific. I just got an interesting tip from an engineer down in the old Colorado Desert. I have it somewhere in all these fool papers. You know the area, of course?"

Stringer answered, "Only that you should cross by rail and at night if possible. It's hot as hell's hinges most of the year and boring all the time. Dead flat and covered with knee-high greasewood as far as the eye can see. I've crossed it a couple of times by rail, but it must have been a pisser to cross in the covered wagon days."

Sam Barca nodded vigorously in assent. "It was. I crossed it that way one time. They called it the Colorado Desert then. Now they're calling it the Imperial Valley and selling it by the full section as prime farm land."

Stringer laughed incredulously. "That's mighty wild, even when you consider bullshit artists like old Wyatt Earp have gone into California real estate of late. I've heard of quick-buck land mongers tying oranges to Joshua trees and selling the whole mess as an orange grove, but there's just no damned way to call those greasewood flats anything but pure desolation. Water holes lie sixty to eighty miles apart down there, and such water as there might be is almost too salty for a mule to drink."

Sam Barca nodded again and growled, "I told you I once crossed that desert—the hard way. Nowadays the tracks avoid the worst part, a big bare salt flat called Salton's Sink—named after a prospector called Salton, by the way. Some geologists hold that the entire area used to be sea bottom. They say many a seashell and an ocean's worth of salt can still be found by sort of shoving the greasewood and lizards out of the way. So that's the news angle."

Stringer shot Barca a bemused look as he queried, "What news angle? That the dead heart of the Colorado

Desert lies betwixt San Diego and Yuma, Sam? Wagon trains following the southern route reported as much back in 1849, for God's sake."

"Shut up and pay attention to your elders," Barca growled. "God has nothing to do with this tale. The Southern Pacific bridged that dry, dusty two or three days of wagon travel with rails a spell this side of '49. To encourage them to do so the government gave 'em the usual railroad grants, every other section or square mile alongside the track in a sort of checkerboard ribbon. The government no doubt figured it could afford to be so generous with public land in the Colorado Desert. It gets two inches of rain in a wet year, and it's so hot even this early in the year that nobody ever had to fight any Indians for it. Creep Huntington had no more use for acres and acres of mummy dust than the Indians. He simply had to lay his tracks across that desert to move his trains on over to Texas. But being an octopus by nature, he naturally accepted every square inch the land office offered."

Stringer blew smoke out both nostrils in bored annoyance and sighed. "Sam, you're still talking ancient history. I've taken that line to Arizona Territory and beyond. I wasn't the only passenger. So I suspect a lot of other folk know there's a railroad across the Colorado Desert now."

Barca snapped, "That's not the whole story. Just keep in mind that the Octopus owns one hell of a lot of flat and fairly fertile desert land, if only it ever rained out yonder." He paused to light an Italian cigar that rather resembled a twisted length of grape vine before he continued. "Around the turn of the century a land speculator called Charley Rockford took a ride on that same railroad. It didn't take him long to notice how much open land there was and that half of it was still free for

the claiming, sun-baked as it might be. So he put together a flim-flam holding company with more than one
name on its stock certificates and a sort of vague mailing address. Then, as soon as he had other men's money
to work with, he enlisted a well-known irrigation engineer named George Chaffey, and put him to work. Then
they dubbed the dead heart of the desert the Imperial
Valley and promised to make the desert bloom like a
rose as they set about selling it off as prime farm land.
Naturally the railroad proceeded to do the same, in cahoots with the quick-buck artists. They had Chaffey run
a diversion canal from the Colorado River out across the
greasewood flats."

Stringer nodded, "Now that you mention it, I recall
some construction going on, over by the Chocolate
Mountains, the last time I passed through. But that was
some time ago, Sam. So I'm still waiting for the news
angle."

Barca blew smoke back at him and explained. "New
homesteads are not news, provided nothing interesting
happens after anyone drills in the first crop. The water
lords and land mongers gave assurance to their suckers
that the irrigated mummy dust of the so-called Imperial
Valley would grow two crops a year of asparagus to
zucchini squash—and maybe it would, given all that
water they promised. But it's easier to promise watering
the desert than to do so."

Barca irritatedly chewed on his half-smoked cigar.
"Things went well enough at first. Chaffey's main
channel was easy enough to dig in soil that's soft as
baby powder. They ran branch lines off to the north and
had close to two thousand settlers and a hundred thousand acres more or less under irrigation within a year or
so. Well, let's say they claimed the 'more' part, but the
settlers say it was a hell of a lot less in their spanking

new Garden of Eden 'cause the irrigation canals silt up almost as fast as they can be dug. The Colorado is one mighty muddy river. It drains mostly higher desert, so it packs at least a quart of solid mud for every gallon of water. And it drops a steamship load of that mud per diem. The whole damned Colorado Desert was spread across the north end of the Gulf of California in the first place by the Colorado and Gila as a sort of combined delta. So in no time at all the main diversion channel wound up full to the brim with fresh dry land."

Stringer whistled softly, then commented, "Leaving all those poor suckers high and dry indeed. Is that the story you want me to cover, boss?"

Barca shook his head. "We ran that last summer, had you paid attention to page three. It gets trickier than that. The water lords and the railroad still have many a dusty desert acre to sell. So as a stopgap, while Chaffey hopes to clean out the main channel, they've subcontracted to run emergency channels on the north and south of the sink. The main diversion channel will drain spring flooding, they hope, south through the Mexican parts of the desert to sea level. Such water would hardly grow much asparagus, of course. So they have another subcontractor running a more modest amount of river water in line with the railroad, feeding the irrigation grid to the north."

Stringer frowned at the rather confused mental map he was forming in his head. "Hold on, Sam. How could they drain river water from the east, which is on its way to the sea, *north* into higher country?"

Barca waved his crooked cigar impatiently and barked, "That's not the mystery. When the mud from the Gila and Colorado spread clean across the upper gulf of California it left a heap of salt water stranded inland. It dried up in no time, forming Salton's Sink which lies a few feet below sea level. The fact that it's a big salt flat is just a fact of nature and has no bearing on the angle I want you to check out. Even an honest irrigation scheme would have to drain north because of the lay of the land out there. And there's no money in trying to sell water or anything else to the few Mexicans down south. Anyways, the irrigation water dries up before it can even make it down to the salt flats, provided there's any water at all. I want you to talk to a man in El Centro about that.''

Barca rummaged again through the papers cluttering his desk until he found the letter he was searching for. He handed it across to Stringer. "Read it later. It's from some gent calling himself Herbert Lockwood. Says he's a hydraulic engineer. In essence the subcontractor he was working for fired him, and he's mad as hell about it. I'd have dismissed it as just another crank letter if I hadn't just heard from the wire service that Chaffey, the head engineer of the whole fool project, has just quit in a huff and walked off the job. He's dropped out of sight, after issuing a statement that the assholes he was working for don't know what they're doing and that he's getting out before things get worse. Since Chaffey failed to say what could be worse than trying to grow crops this coming spring with no water, we can only hope this other browned-off hydraulic engineer, Lockwood, might be able to tell us, and that there's a story in it somewhere for the paper. By us I mean you, of course. Even if I wasn't busy in this box, rank has its privileges and the desert down yonder will be hotter than I like, even this early in the year.''

Stringer snuffed out the remains of his own smoke and raised one eyebrow. "I always suspected you loved me, Sam," he drawled ironically. "Anyway, the desert's not that bad in late winter if you dress sensible. And how do I find this Lockwood gent once I get to El Centro?"

"You ask, of course," Barca retorted. "He sent his letter of complaint via General Delivery, El Centro. And while El Centro seems to be the county seat, you can likely shout his name from any rooftop with a fair chance of his hearing you. The town is little more than a Southern Pacific water stop. Wire me by Western Union as soon as you find out what's going on down there."

As Stringer rose, he asked, "And what if nothing's going on?"

Barca replied in a disgusted tone, "Come back without wasting money on any damned wire, of course. Western Union charges us a nickel a word, you know."

Stringer nodded and observed morosely, "I know. I sure wish I could get you to pay me that much a word, you tight-fisted old cuss."

CHAPTER
TWO

The day's ride down to Los Angeles was tedious. Although Stringer had dressed more comfortably for field work in his jeans and blue denim jacket, he'd left his gun rig packed out of sight in his gladstone traveling bag. But he got stared at anyway by fellow passengers who acted as if they'd never seen a beat-up Rough Rider hat or spurred Justins before. Stringer managed to amuse himself during the boring journey by philosophizing how surprising as well as somewhat discomforting it was to consider how sissified the West Coast had become in the past few years.

Stringer decided it was too late to catch the night train to San Diego, where he would get the connection to El Centro the next day. So he booked a room at the hotel across from the Union Depot. Then, seeing it was too early to turn in, he hired a worn-out bay gelding and an even older stock saddle at a nearby livery to ride out to the new suburb of Hollywoodland. He'd been invited to visit more than once by his old acquaintance Wyatt

Earp. More importantly, though, while he took some of old Wyatt's frontier yarns with a grain of salt, he needed the savvy of a real estate agent right now. And whatever he might or might not have been in Tombstone, Wyatt Earp was said to be a pisser of a real estate agent.

Stringer found the old windbag with his latest and much-younger wife, Sarah, rocking on the porch of their bungalow off Western Avenue. While the pretty brunette worked on her needlepoint, the former fron-tiersman was cleaning a Winchester as if he expected buffalo to stampede up the paved street any minute.

The old lawman and his lovely but flutter-brained wife had met Stringer up in Nome during the Alaska Gold Rush and had run across him a time or two in the current century, and now they both greeted him like long-lost kin. As he tethered his hired mount to their picket fence, Sarah dropped her needlework and ran across the Bermuda grass to give him a big and not too sisterly hug. Old Wyatt didn't seem to mind though, and as he put his gun and cleaning tools aside he called out, "You just missed supper. But we can coffee and cake you, MacKail. You'll be staying the night, of course."

Stringer joined his gracious host on the porch, with his gracious hostess still clinging to him like a cockle burr. He shook his head and replied, "Not hardly, thanks just the same. I'm bound for the Colorado Desert—or Imperial Valley, take your choice—to see if I can find out what's going on over there. Being I'm between trains, I thought I'd ask for the words of an expert on dry and dusty real estate, Mister Earp."

The old-timer responded, "Call me Wyatt and don't make rude remarks about Hollywoodland. You see that line of genuine palm trees over yonder? They get wa-tered regular, and our neighbor two doors down has a real lemon tree growing in his back garth. Ain't that a bitch?"

Stringer turned to stare dubiously at what looked more like a line of giant feather dusters with their handles buried in the white gravel of the Los Angeles Basin. Then he shrugged diplomatically. "They must be young palms, if you say so. I can't come up with anything else that grows so silly. Ain't palm trees supposed to have trunks, though?"

Wyatt Earp sniffed. "Give 'em time. My point is that they've taken root. Dang near anything will grow in this fine climate as long as you can get some water to it."

Sarah Earp untangled herself from Stringer to announce she had a gardening book she was working on and ran in the house, apparently to fetch it for him. Stringer sat on the steps near the old lawman's rocker and got out the makings as he explained the little he knew about events in the desert to the southeast.

When he'd finished, Wyatt Earp pursed his lips and said, "I don't know, son. I once drove a stage over yonder in Salton's Sink. It never struck me as prime farm or even grazing land. Come high summer it gets too hot for buzzards to even fly over. You say the Southern Pacific owns that stretch of mummy sweat?"

"Half of it, leastways," Stringer explained. "I reckon old C. P. Huntington was in a hurry to lay his tracks across that hellish stretch and just took the land titles because they came free."

Earp nodded sagely and agreed. "Creep Huntington was a greedy son of a bitch. Did I ever tell you about the time I shot it out with his hired guns at Mussel Slough, boy?"

Stringer acknowledged he had heard the story before, but added slyly, "You sure must have been a traveling man in those days, Wyatt, considering what you say you did at the O. K. Corral in Tombstone a year later."

Earp smiled modestly. "Me and my brother, Morgan, spent a lot of time on the road riding shotgun for Wells Fargo."

Stringer knew better. But he'd been raised to be respectful of his elders, so he just said, "I'd rather talk about Salton's Sink. Is it true we're talking about a lot of salt spread over the garden spot of the Colorado Desert, Wyatt?"

The older man chuckled. "Enough salt to scrape up off the dirt and sprinkle in your stew, if you don't mind a bit of grit. Of course, the salt's only that bad in the low places. I reckon you could get prickly pear or even mesquite to grow in the higher greasewood ground if you could get water to it now and again." He pointed at a distant greenish blur a few streets over. "That's a genuine pepper tree, yonder. Comes all the way from South America. You see, we do have some water, here. It runs down offen the Santa Monica Mountains a month or more each winter and settles here under the basin, not all that deep."

Stringer repressed a shrug of impatience as he insisted, "I know there's a real estate boom in this basin, Wyatt. It's all that land up for sale to the southeast that has me puzzled. I've been hearing all my life how good the late C. P. Huntington was at squeezing blood out of stones and . . ."

"That's the pure truth," Wyatt Earp cut in. "There never was and never will be a skinflint bastard like old Creep Huntington. He'd have skinned his own mother if there'd been a bounty on old lady hides. But he can't be skinning nobody over in the desert now. The old son of a bitch up and died on us all afore anyone could draw a good bead on him!"

Stringer said, "That's my point. Whether you listen

to his few friends or his many enemies, C. P. Huntington was one hell of a businessman. So how come, while he was still alive and in business, it never occurred to him to make that desert blossom and sell off at least the half he owned for hard cash? Hell, he peddled lots of semi-arid land in his time. Some of it is still piss poor. Wouldn't you say that had he thought he could peddle that salty desert land without serving time as an out-and-out swindler, he'd have done so?"

Wyatt Earp nodded thoughtfully and considered some before he decided. "You're right. There are some limits to what we consider safe to sell, even to green-horns. I just had a look at some mighty cheap tidal flats down south of Santa Monica. It looks a lot like a green grassy meadow, when the tide is out. But I dunno, I don't think I'd want to defend myself in court for selling city lots that spend part of every day under the Pacific Ocean. Maybe the slickers who took over after old Creep died ain't as ethical as you and me or even old Creep Huntington."

Earp's young wife came back just in time to hear her husband's last remark. As she sat down on the steps to place the tray she'd fetched from the house between herself and Stringer, she screwed her pretty face into a pout. "They're just horrid, all mean and stuck-up. Wyatt and me never got an invite to their grand house-warming over in Pasadena. But we went anyway, figuring they just hadn't heard my famous husband had moved to these parts after taming Nome that time. I have never in this world been treated so rude before."

From his rocker, Earp explained. "They turned us away at the gate. A snooty butler did, I mean. I told the cuss I'd once lost at cards to old Creep Huntington and that it only stood to reason his nephew Hank would be proud to show us about his grand new mansion. But it was like talking to a block of ice. So me and my Sarah decided to let 'em hold their fool party without the honor of our presence."

"Wyatt's real famous here in Hollywoodland," Sarah pointed out as she put aside the loose-leaf folder she'd brought out with the coffee and dessert to cut Stringer a heroic slice of lemon cake.

Her husband nodded in argeement. "I get paid real money to go over moving picture scripts for some eastern dudes who just went into business up Western Avenue. Say, would you like to have a part in a Wild West nickelodeon, Stringer? All you have to know is how to ride a bronc, and you're already dressed more cow than half the nickelodeon cowboys I've seen. Before they called on me to show 'em the ropes they had the dangdest remuda of oddly dressed riders you ever seen. Some of 'em even reported for work in English riding habits and posted in flat saddles like they was out hunting foxes instead of outlaws."

Stringer almost choked on lemon cake as he tried to laugh and swallow at the same time. He washed the errant bite of cake down with coffee, gasped for breath, and allowed, "I can see why they'd feel the need for your memories of an older west, Wyatt."

He was too polite to point out that features he'd written for the *Sun* had called for a certain amount of research on his own part and, what the hell, old Wyatt had at least been through Dodge and Tombstone in his time, even if it had been mostly as a card dealer and cat-house bouncer. He assured the well-meaning Wyatt that he wasn't interested in becoming a nickelodeon star. Then, returning to his own immediate interest, he asked, "If this Henry Huntington who took over for his dead uncle is living as high on the hog as you say, might that not explain all the sudden interest in mongering desert land that even the one and original Octopus had written off as useless?"

Earp shrugged. "Old Creep would have likely sold his worn-out socks if he'd figured there was a market for 'em. Young Hank acts a lot more social and sissy. But he's got the same blood in him, even if he is trying to pretend it's blue."

Sarah refilled Stringer's cup as she remarked, "He just bought that famous painting—I think he calls it 'The Blue Boy'—to make folk think him and his fancy wife hail from fancier parts, as if they were ashamed of being plain old Americans like the rest of us."

Wyatt Earp scowled and added, "But unlike the rest of us plain old Americans, they never done an honest day's work in their lives. Old Creep Huntington had his bad habits and spitting tobacco was the least of 'em. But to give the devil his due, old Creep built a railroad empire from the ground up with little more than poker stakes and a mess of Chinamen. I don't see where young Hank gets any right to play so high and mighty with his fancy ways and big house full of old oil paintings. It ain't as if he made the money or even drove one railroad spike on his own." Earp shook his head. "Nossir. You just leave me and my little Sarah that much money, free and clear, for doing nothing and we'll surely show you how to live like royalty. It can't be all that hard."

Sarah clapped her hands like the child she really was inside her beautiful head and giggled. "Oh, wouldn't that be fun? If I was Mrs. Huntington I'd have the biggest house and garden in Southern California, and invite all the neighbors in."

She saw Stringer had finished his somewhat overly sweet repast and reached for her folder, saying, "I want to show you my latest literary effort, Mister MacKail. You being a famous author and all."

Stringer had no choice but to take the tome from her and open it, braced for anything. He saw to his relief that half the manuscript seemed to be pictures, hand-drawn in crayon and not too badly at that. Facing each floral illustration was a page of her self-consciously neat handwriting. When she asked him what he thought of it, Stringer said, "You sure know a lot about flowers, ma'am. But weren't you working on your husband's bi-ography the last time we met?"

She dimpled charmingly. "Oh, I finished that one. I titled it 'Me and Wyatt Earp' and sent it to Boston to be published. I haven't heard from them one way or the other yet."

From his rocker her older husband chuckled fondly down at her. "I doubt she ever will," he told Stringer. "She writ it a mite more flattersome than historical. I keep telling the dear woman I never shot Curly Bill. But she doesn't listen."

Sarah retorted firmly, "Pooh, if you didn't shoot that nasty man who did? He's dead, isn't he?"

Wyatt Earp didn't answer. Neither did Stringer. It was nice to hear that tall story hadn't come from the old lawman himself. It might have been impolite to report that Curly Bill Brocius had been seen alive and well a full ten years after the Earps had been run out of Tomb-stone, as pests, by Sheriff John Slaughter.

To return the conversation to safer ground, Stringer turned a page of Sarah's book and admired the spray of yucca blooms she'd drawn. As he leafed through the book, he addressed Wyatt. "Do you have Henry Hun-tington's Pasadena address on hand, in case I've time to interview him before I move on to his land of milk and honey in Salton's Sink?"

Earp shook his head. "House that big don't need to have numbers out front. You just ask anyone in Pasadena where the grandest house in town might be and they'll just naturally point." Then he added, "Won't do you no good, though. That new Huntington palace is laid out as if they was expecting bill collectors and Apache all at once. The house is set way back from the gate and they got a sort of prison wall wrapped around the whole spread."

"Don't they have a door chime?" asked Stringer.

"Sure they do," his host replied with a snort. "I rung it personal that time. All you get from your effort is a sort of sissy-dressed but mighty big dude looking down at you to say you can't come in. Entrance is by written invite only. I was dressed a lot more refined than you are right now and they still acted as if they feared I'd spit on the Persian rugs and carve my initials in a marble wall. Why in thunder would you want to talk to such a snooty rascal as Hank Huntington to begin with?"

Stringer answered thoughtfully, "For openers, he might know what the devil the Southern Pacific is up to down in Salton's Sink. All I have to go on is the word of a fired and no doubt disgruntled employee who may or may not be in El Centro, miles from whatever's really going on. I'd like to hear the Southern Pacific's side of the story before jumping to any conclusions."

"That sounds fair," Earp commented. "But hold on. I might be able to save you a long ride to Pasadena."

He got up and went inside, long enough for his young wife to shyly ask Stringer what he thought of her gardening book and have him tell her, truthfully enough, that she sure drew right nicely. Then old Wyatt came back out with a sheaf of real estate brochures. "These come in the mail awhile back. I reckon they

figured all the local real estate agents would be interested. I'd almost forgotten I had 'em."

Earp sat this time on the steps with his wife and their
visitor and handed the lithographed promotion pieces to
Stringer. "Anyone can see how dumb the pictures are,
unless they never had the pleasure of crossing the Colorado Desert in summer."

Stringer had to agree as he scanned through the uto-
pian plans of the Southern Pacific Land Office. Even if
they somehow, someday, managed to get water out to
the middle of those greasewood flats, orange groves and
paved tree-shaded roads seemed just a mite optimistic.
The architect's renderings of planned communities in
Spanish-mission style were better, as art work, than
Sarah Earp's crayon drawings but a hell of a lot less
realistic. For at least the lady had sketched flowers that
existed rather than just letting her imagination run riot.
The railroad grants for sale were listed at a price
cheaper—but only barely—than prime farm land in the
fertile Sacramento Valley to the north, and they sold at a
minimum of a quarter section.

Stringer searched for any mention of water rates.
Finding none, he told Earp, "I just can't see it. Seems to
me that if I wanted to grow barley instead of cows I'd
pay a few bucks an acre more for a proven farmstead up
near, say, Weed or Red Bluff where I'd get my water for
the price of a tube well."

Earp nodded, then opined, "You'd have to drill in
crops more profitsome than barley to make a go of it
with hired water. It just don't pay to irrigate grain and
grazing land. As to all the orange trees they seem to be
promising, I can get you a cheaper price on an already
planted grove down in Orange County to the south.
You'll never guess why they named it Orange County
'til you see how many orange trees they got growing

down yonder this very minute. I told you I chucked these offers aside as soon as I took one look at 'em."

Stringer searched for an office address, found one on Main Street not far from his downtown hotel, and asked if he could keep that particular page. Earp said he was welcome to the whole bundle but asked slyly how much salty desert land he meant to buy.

Stringer explained. "I'm not ready to tell anyone I'm a newspaperman until they tell me where all that water's supposed to come from, or how much they'll be charging an acre-foot for it. I find it sort of suspicious that they've left that out, considering how carefully they drew all these thirsty orange and shade trees."

Earp agreed that a land swindle would be nothing new for the old Southern Pacific. Nevertheless, Stringer knew there was no real story in such standard real estate practices, and after some more polite small talk he excused himself to remount his hired pony and ride like hell for downtown L. A. in hopes of finding the land office still open.

It was downhill most of the way, no more than six or seven miles across mostly vacant lots. But when he got there he found that he'd abused his livery mount needlessly. A sign in the window said they stayed open until 9:00 P.M. to serve the world slices of the Imperial Valley pie.

Stringer tethered his jaded pony to the hitching post out front and went on in, spurs ringing and a stub of Bull Durham smouldering between his lips. He didn't outright say he was a hayseed. But as he'd often pointed out to Sam Barca, a newspaper man was sometimes able to get more out of a slicker by looking not half as slick.

A pretty young gal behind the counter asked what she could do for him. He allowed he was interested in the land her outfit might be opening up for settlement in the Imperial Valley. So she led him back to a slicker indeed, seated behind an acre or so of glass-topped desk. The land monger offered Stringer a soft leather seat, puffed on his own expensive cigar, and asked how much of the ground floor Stringer wanted to get in on at these once in a lifetime prices.

Stringer said, "To tell the truth, pard, the offering a pal of mine just showed me said more about future trees than present water. If I was to spring for, say, a full section, just what might it cost me to irrigate the same?"

The land monger looked pained. Then he leaned forward, as if fearing one of his fellow slickers might overhear, and confided in a sincere tone, "The Southern Pacific only sells the land. The canals from the Colorado River are being dug by a water syndicate, see?"

Stringer frowned and tried to put more country in his own sincerity as he replied, "Not hardly. Seems to me I'd be buying a pig in a poke, and then some, if I went for bone-dry land at any price. What if that other outfit fails to deliver in the end? What would I ever do with a section of greasewood flats, pray for rain?"

The S.P. agent said, "I can see you know a thing or two about land speculation, Mister MacKail. Putting all our cards on the table, I will tell you true that the Southern Pacific offers no guarantee you'll ever grow a head of lettuce on the land we're offering so cheap. I don't mind saying the lots we're offering may be worth less than nothing should the water project fail. We've been paying taxes for years on land we couldn't give away before the engineers discovered a canal route from the Colorado River near Yuma to the center of the Imperial Valley and beyond. We're not affiliated with the water outfit in any way. But we know them by reputation and we think we know a good plan when we see one."

Stringer nodded doubtfully. "So why ain't the grand irrigation scheme on paper, where a body like me could judge for himself whether they know their asses from their elbows?"

"That's simple," the S. P. agent answered, smiling thinly. "We'd look dumb mapping water canals on our own brochures when we're not sure where they'll run in the end, wouldn't we? The Imperial Valley is flat as a pancake to the eye, but water runs a lot more particular. They have to grade their canals as they go, to allow for such gentle rolling as there might be to the lay of the land, see?"

Stringer shifted the unlit stub of his smoke to the far side of his mouth and replied, "I dunno. I suspect I'd best have me a powwow with these water lords afore I lay out any hard-earned cash. How do I go about that? Do they have an office somewhere around here pard?"

The slicker shook his head and tried to look regretful. "Nope. Yuma, in the Arizona Territory, is where they have their main office. They may or may not be able to show you just how far any land you buy off us may wind up from one of their main feeder canals. The point you seem to be missing is that now is the time to grab some of that cheap land, before the real land rush starts. Irrigated desert loam can run as high as three figures an acre. Would you rather buy a full section at those prices?"

Stringer said, "Not hardly," and got to his feet. "I reckon I'd best study on it some. It's been nice talking to you."

The land monger didn't argue. He was no doubt used to having anyone with the brains of a gnat hesitate to jump at the chance to buy a greasewood flat. And that would have been the end of it had not Stringer encountered yet another slicker coming in as he was leaving.

Stringer didn't recall the man's face. But the son of a bitch shot him a thoughtful look and demanded, "Say, aren't you Stuart Mackail from the *San Francisco Sun?* What brings you to our land office at this hour, for Pete's sake?"

Stringer muttered he'd come to see Pete and pushed past him and out to the street, his impersonation of a sucker blown to shreds. But, what the hell, he'd likely found out as much as these land mongers meant to tell anyone in any case.

CHAPTER
THREE

Downtown L. A. had grown up around the already fair-sized Pueblo de Los Angeles, and nobody had evicted the original Hispanic population as other ethnic groups moved in. This didn't worry Stringer until he'd returned his hired mount to the livery and found himself afoot on the dark sidestreet a livery hand had assured him to be the shortest way to his hotel.

The buildings to either side were frame. Mexican carpenters had been as quick to grasp the advantages of the Yankee two-by-four and machine-made nail as anyone else in the Los Angeles Basin. So Chicano kids were taking advantage of that other Anglo cultural introduction, the front porch, to lie in wait for any source of amusement that might pass through their otherwise dull thoroughfair. As a native Californian himself, Stringer spoke a more refined Spanish, or surely a more polite form, than he heard in passing. But since his .38 was packed in his gladstone and he'd left the goddamned travel bag in his hotel room, he thought it wiser to pretend he didn't understand some of the remarks he heard about his hat, his mother, and obvious sexual orientation.

He'd just about made it back to the more brightly lit and more populated Main Street around Union Depot when he heard a feminine scream behind him. He knew it was dumb to look back in a neighborhood like this one, but the lady in distress sounded sincere. So he turned just in time to see a teenaged Chicano jogging his way, laughing, with the purse he'd snatched in one hand and the knife he'd used to cut the carrying strap in the other. Stringer couldn't make out his victim at the end of the darkened street, but her voice came loud and clear as she called out, "Stop, thief! Oh, lord, somebody stop that thief!"

So Stringer stopped him, knife and all, by stepping aside as a prudent gent in these parts was supposed to, and then rabbit-punching the purse snatcher as he passed.

The Chicano youth belly-flopped to the brick wall and stayed there, moaning soft and low, as Stringer scooped up the eight-inch knife and purloined purse. He'd just risen back to full height when a lady ran up to him, gasping. "That's my purse, sir."

He handed it to her, saying, "I noticed. Now stick tight as a tick and we'll see if this is over yet."

It wasn't. As Stringer and what he now saw to be a pretty young miss in a travel duster and straw boater atop her pinned-up hair moved on toward the brighter lights, a trio of Chicano toughs who'd cat-footed it down the other side of the dark street suddenly darted across to block their way. The girl made the mistake of stopping, forcing Stringer to do the same. This gave two others who'd been tagging behind time to get into the act. The girl was trying not to cry as she clung to

Stringer's left arm. Stringer didn't feel at all like crying, but he didn't feel too optimistic either.

"Let go my arm and let me handle this, ma'am," he muttered to the terrified girl.

One of the gang snickered, then said, "That's right, puta, let the big caballero handle us. Didn't you know any gringo can take on any number of us poor greasers?"

In her fear, the girl couldn't answer, and Stringer saw no reason to. It was the usual set-up for a street gang. He knew the one doing all the talking was the last one he had to keep an eye on. Once they worked themselves up, it was usually the biggest bozo in the gang who'd wade in first.

The talker seemed to feel it was his duty to draw more of a response from them, so he asked Stringer, "Hey, vaquero, where is your horse? Do the putas of your kind admire big hats and spurs on a shop clerk? For why did you take the side of this one, here? Are not the girls of this barrio good enough for you?"

Stringer smiled thinly, not taking his eyes from the bigger one to the left of their tormentor as he answered, in Spanish, "I have never seen your mother. So you would know better than I whether she is any good in bed or not. Why don't you trot her out and let us have a look at her if you are pimping for her?"

The spokesman gasped in stunned indignation while some of the others laughed in spite of themselves. But as Stringer had so wisely assumed, it was the big one who growled, "That is no way to speak about my friend's mother." Then, as the muscle of the gang interposed his bulk between Stringer and their offended taunter, Stringer grabbed the girl's elbow with his left hand and charged first, the knife blade in his right fist coming up low and dirty to rip the big one's guts from groin to breastbone.

The bully of the bunch could see he meant it, as he leaped backwards with a chicken squawk to land a good six feet back. Another gang member made a hesitant move toward Stringer from his right, and Stringer slashed his shirt and some belly fat before he too crawfished back through a picket fence, bleating, *"Hijo de puerca!* You cut me!"

Stringer snapped, "My mistake. I was out to kill you." He dragged the now sobbing Anglo girl straight at the gang's leader. The big one had his own knife out by now, but there was something about Stringer's direct approach, wielding a blade he obviously knew how to use, that induced him to yell, *"Vamanos, muchachos! El gringo es loco en la cabeza!"*

And so, having dismissed him as a deranged foreigner, the gang evaporated, perhaps to reconsider, and Stringer ran with the girl all the way to the entrance of his hotel on the far side of the encouraging street lamps. He looked back in time to see just a shift of movement in the darkness they'd just left. So he hauled her inside the dimly lit vestibule, explaining, "We may not be out of the woods yet. We'd best fort up a spell before I run you home. Where might that be, Miss . . . ah?"

She gasped, "I'm Zelda Gordon and you'd be . . . ?"

"Stuart MacKail and I'd have never saved you if I'd known you hailed from an enemy clan," he replied with a reassuring chuckle, but she didn't seem to get it. One no doubt had to be exposed to good old Uncle Don MacKail to have a grasp of the clan feuds in the old country, he decided.

"Never mind," he assured her. "Us Scotch-Americans have to stick together in any case. What on earth were you doing in Little Mexico just now and where do you want to wind up tonight?"

"I was on my way to the railroad depot," she answered. "I'm bound for my home in San Diego after visiting my sister and her new baby in Glendale. A nice Mexican girl I asked for directions told me that street back there was a shortcut."

He grimaced and replied, "She sure must have liked you. All right, I see the picture now. Your best bet is a hack ride back to your sister's place, once we're sure the coast is clear. You'll have just missed the night train to San Diego. I know because I missed it on purpose. It would have put me in San Diego late at night, with another train to change to around noon tomorrow. I figured as long as I had to lay over I might as well check in here. Had a few bases here in L. A. to cover and I don't know anyone in San Diego . . . then."

She said, "Oh dear, I don't want to go all the way back to Glendale and have my sister weep farewell at me all over again. You say you have a room here and that we'd both be on our way south aboard the same morning train?"

He nodded. "I did. Do you want me to see if we could book you a room? It's not a bad old hotel. Mayhaps a mite shabby. But it smells clean and the last time I stayed here I failed to spy any bugs."

She looked undecided and rummaged through the purse he'd saved for her. "I suppose that would be most practical," she murmured. "But I only came up here for a short visit that kept me longer than I'd planned. How much do they charge here for a small room with no trimmings?"

"I'm not sure," Stringer answered. "I booked one with a bath for a dollar a night. Why don't we talk to the room clerk inside?"

She nodded dubiously, and he led her into the murky lobby. They'd turned down the lights and, except for one old man dozing under a rubber plant in a corner, the place seemed empty. Stringer led Zelda over to the deserted front desk and rang the bell on the mock-marble top. Nobody answered even after several rings. Behind him, Zelda suddenly gasped and said, "Oh, lordy, I think those Mexicans have followed us!"

He turned to follow her gaze. There seemed to be no signs of life out front right now, but then the glass of the front door was grimed as well as distant. Zelda suggested anxiously, "Why don't we go on up, for now, and you can ask at the desk later."

That sounded sensible, and besides, Stringer was just beginning to notice that her hair was a soft lowland brown and her eyes were big and blue. He helped her up the stairs to the second floor and led her to his corner room. Fortunately, he'd held on to his hotel key, knowing that few hotel clerks cared anyway since it saved them work.

As he led her in and switched on the overhead Edison bulb, Zelda glanced about admiringly. "Oh, this is much nicer than I expected, Stuart."

He didn't know what she'd been expecting. The room had cross-ventilation and an adjoining bath, but it was otherwise sort of seedy to his way of thinking. The wallpaper was ugly unless one admired orange flowers that Sarah Earp could have drawn better in crayon, and the only light fixture that didn't seem to be burnt out was the one in the ceiling above the brass bedstead. A fake Tiffany lamp sat atop a gateleg table near one window, and some earlier guest had stolen the clothes hooks in the one tiny closet. Stringer waved at the door to the bath in case his unexpected guest wanted to wash her hands or whatever. Then he pulled down the shades for such privacy as they offered from the world outside and plopped his Rough Rider atop the table lamp, the most suitable way in a strange hotel room to his way of thinking of getting his hat off his head while making it not too tough to find it in the future.

As he turned, he saw Zelda seated on the bed, fooling with the severed strap of the purse she'd almost lost.

"I can square-knot that for you if you like," he offered. "It won't look all that grand. But at least you'll be able to hang it from your shoulder 'til you can get to a decent shoemaker."

She thought that was a fine notion and, as he sat down beside her, she unbuttoned her duster, revealing the print dress underneath. Stringer carefully helped her out of her coat. Then, because there were no clothes hooks in the closet, he took it over to the same table lamp, lifted his hat, and draped the poplin duster neatly over the domed lamp shade before he replaced his hat atop everything.

Zelda laughed, commenting that it looked like a little old man seated there. Then Stringer went back to the bed, sat down, and returned to work on her purse strap. She told him, as she watched, that he had clever hands. He didn't answer. He'd already noticed her hands but didn't think it would have been polite to comment on the paler ring of flesh around the third finger of her left hand. A gal had a right to remove her wedding band for whatever reason, and he wasn't up to hearing long, sad stories about such matters unless the folk involved were famous enough to rate a scandal column in the *Sun*.

He'd just fashioned a small secure knot and trimmed it even neater with his pocketknife when a windowpane shattered and something buzzed just above their heads to thunk into the wall above the head of the bed.

Stringer shoved Zelda flat and sprang the other way

to flip the light switch near the door. As the room was plunged in darkness, he heard her gasp, "What was that, a rock through the window?"

He told her to stay down as he moved toward the window in a crouch. Then he saw the bullet hole in the drawn shade, and he had to grope about on the floor near the table before he found his hat and her travel duster spread across the floor with the remains of the table lamp.

"I'd say somebody just shot at me as I was sitting by the window, outlined against the shade," he said. "I sure hope it looked that way to whoever had it in for me, don't you?"

She sat up, despite his orders. "Oh, lord, it must have been those Mexicans!"

He answered thoughtfully, "Maybe. If they'd had a gun handy back there, we'd have had more trouble getting away from 'em. Of course, one of 'em could have gone home to borrow his papacito's hunting rifle. But this time, I don't know. . . ."

He moved back to the bed to reach under it for his gladstone and haul it out. Their eyes had adjusted to the street glow from outside by now, so she was able to see what he was up to as he got out his gun rig and hung it over a bedpost with the grips of his S&W Double Action handy.

She asked soberly, "Do you think they'll really come all the way inside?"

He tried to sound reassuring as he bolted the door. "I doubt it. If they think they got me they'll want to put a heap of distance between themselves and the scene of their crime."

He sat beside her again. There was no other furniture worth sitting on in the little room. She suddenly wrapped both arms around him and pleaded, "Oh, hold me! I'm so scared, Stuart!"

Being a gentleman, he did. He wasn't holding her at all sassy, but he could still tell she wasn't wearing whalebone or much of anything else under her thin frock. Her straw boater had fallen off and her hair smelled of lavender shampoo as she held her cheek to his chest and went on shivering like a frightened pup. He held her tighter and kissed the bare nape of her neck as he soothed, "There, there, it's likely over. I don't suspect anyone else in the place even noticed. We'll just sit tight a spell and then, once we're sure it's over, I'll go on down and see about a room for you, okay?"

She sobbed, "I don't want you to leave me alone in this horrid town for a second! Why can't I just stay here with you for the night?"

He hesitated, then pointed out, "For openers, there's just this one bed, Miss Zelda."

She said, "I know. But I can leave my chemise on and it will be dark and . . . well, don't you think you could be trusted if we each stayed on our own side all night?"

He sighed and answered truthfully. "Nope. I could mayhaps manage to behave that platonic if you had two heads and both of 'em ugly. But to tell the truth, I find it sort of tough to behave myself now with you in the dark, fully dressed atop the covers. So we're going to have to study on bedding you down safer somewhere else, unless you'd like to see me make a total fool of myself."

She sighed and said, "Oh dear, there seems to be only one practical way to deal with this awkward situation then."

He agreed and, as she rose to her feet, he assumed she meant her words more properly than her next action showed. There was no mistaking her meaning, though, once she started to climb out of her duds. There was enough light for him to stare up at her, slack-jawed, as she tossed her shimmy shirt aside to rejoin him, naked as a jay, atop the covers.

It didn't take Stringer long to shuck his own duds and get the two of them under the covers. But she was still imploring, "Hurry! Please don't tease me so!" by the time he was in her with a pillow under her rollicking rump and, though he rode her to glory with more than a little enthusiasm, Zelda climaxed ahead of him—twice —and begged for more as he lay gasping for his second wind atop her firm naked breasts. As she wrapped her strong slender thighs around him to hug him closer, Stringer knew he'd been right about that wedding band she'd shucked. He didn't want to know whether an extremely enthusiastic marriage had ended in some unfortunate manner or whether she was just a married gal who traveled incognito away from home. So he didn't ask. They made love again, and then again, before she had mercy on him and gave him a chance to roll a smoke and cuddle her more calmly for a spell.

By this time she'd calmed down enough, if she'd ever really been that scared, to ask once more about the rifle shot that had brought them together so romantically. He took a thoughtful drag of Bull Durham and told her, "It works two ways. The obvious way could have been a grouchy Chicano, as I mentioned before. On the other hand, I'm a fairly well-known newspaperman who's written more than one exposé on crooked dealings. Just before we met I'd been nosing about a mayhaps crooked land office, and they'd just figured out who I really was as I was leaving."

She said that sounded confusing but thrilling, so he wound up telling her the story of his life in the condensed version he used for such pillow conversations. He found it no more tedious than to listen to the self-serving tales that gals seemed to feel situations like this called for. He'd never seen why folk needed excuses to go to bed together. It surely had sleeping alone beat all hollow.

When he'd finished his tale and even shorter smoke, Zelda went on combing his belly hairs with her nails, purring, "Well, I never would have taken you for a newspaperman, dear. You look and talk so . . . well, out-doorsy. I thought you were a rancher or something."

He sighed, then answered, "Yeah, for some reason I have to explain that to half the grammar school graduates I meet up with. They pay me to write educated English with all the spelling and punctuation right. I just told you how I worked my way through Stanford by herding cows part-time. Anyways, nobody talks as formal as they write. How often do you reckon Sir Walter Scott used *Thee* and *Thou* in normal conversation with his kith and kin? I was born and reared in the Mother Lode country amid folk who talked cow unless they talked Spanish or Miwok. You ought to hear old Jack London talk some time. Come to think on it, your pretty little ears might be too delicate."

She gasped, "Heavens! Do you know the famous Jack London, the author of *Call of the Wild*?"

"We met up in Frisco as rival cub reporters," Stringer grimaced. "He's still a fair newspaperman. It's those potboiling novels he's taken to writing that are full of bull. Fancy as he writes, old Jack was a product of the Frisco Bay mudflats. He grew up Shanty Irish and got to be more famous as an oyster pirate than anything else until he discovered, in jail, he had a knack for writing. He's yet to learn to spell. But that's why editors were born, so it don't show by the time those fancy words he can't even pronounce show up in print. Old Sam Clemens, now—you probably know him as Mark Twain —is just the opposite. He talks like an educated gentleman and writes like a Mississippi deck hand. You can't judge a book by its cover or expect a writer to sound like he writes, unless he's reading you his own stuff, see?"

Zelda seemed to have become bored with all this talk of literary style. She yawned politely and moved her hand further down. When she inquired if he had his second wind yet, he allowed he had and rolled back in the saddle, saying with a friendly chuckle, "Open the chute and let's see if I can stay aboard this bronc."

She laughed like hell at his remark, showing that she appreciated his style, and then she bucked even harder.

So, all in all, his layover in L. A. was mighty enjoyable—as long as it was safe to assume nobody was out seriously to kill him that is.

CHAPTER
FOUR

The dinky, dusty town of El Centro made Stringer glad he'd shared that last bath with the amazing Zelda before they'd parted. His teeth were gritty and his shirt collar felt grimy by the time he'd toted his gladstone from the sun-baked railroad platform to the nearest shade. Despite Sam Barca's observation that it was early in the year for real heat in these parts, it was already hot enough. The town was surrounded by dead-flat miles of nothing much. El Centro was so small he could see outside it by peering down any street. A few of the buildings were badly built adobes, although most were boomtown frame. The soil underfoot was a sort of talcum powder silt that didn't make for firm 'dobe bricks no matter how much straw and cow shit was mixed in with it. He spied a sign in the middle distance offering beer or Coca Cola, both on ice. So he spat out some liquid mud and headed that way.

As he did so, a one-horse hearse and some dusty Mexicans playing a funeral dirge passed him, headed the other way. Stringer idly assumed they meant to either bury the poor cuss farther out amid the slate-blue greasewood clumps or, just as likely, put the body on the next train through. If that was their intention, he could only hope they'd used plenty of embalming fluid. Trains ran few and far between along this stretch of the Southern Pacific. The track drifted south of the official border past Mexicali, but nobody seemed to care. Anyone aiming to cross the border unlawfully in these parts would have to be mighty ambitious as well as half camel. For unless and until that irrigation project ever got here, there wasn't another water hole for many a dusty mile, north or south. A lazy daisy windmill back by the trackside water tower announced the presence of ground water, deep under the chalky surface. The railroad had apparently built the drab little settlement as a water stop for its thirsty locomotives. No matter where in the world they wandered, a steam train had to jerk water every hundred miles or so.

Stringer entered the dinky saloon and put down his bag. He'd strapped his gun on before getting down from the cross-country train, but there was hardly anyone in the place to mind. The saloon was store-front wide and about forty feet back, with the bar along one of the longer walls. The other wall was lined with tables and chairs, all painted an electric blue in the Mexican manner. Some said the color repelled flies, and that may have been why the flies in the saloon were circling a strip of flypaper at the far end of the bar. The old-timer mopping the other end with a damp rag asked Stringer to name his pleasure. He said he'd drink just about anything that was cold and wet, but he was still a mite surprised when the barkeep served him a bottle of Coca Cola, saying, "You may as well help me get rid of this stuff then. Hardly any of my regular customers seem to like it since Teddy Roosevelt made 'em take the cocaine outten Coca Cola. Nothing to it now but cola-nut juice and sugar water. They'll likely be going out of business any day now."

Stringer was too thirsty to argue. He guzzled half the bottle at one gulp, belched, and observed, "Sure tastes better than your topsoil."

The old-timer chuckled. "Oh, the soil ain't so bad, this far to the south. Goes from good loam to pure alkali as you ride north into Salton's Sink."

"If you say so," Stringer said, sipping some more soda pop. "I'd hate to try to grow serious weeds out there though."

The old barkeep nodded. "So would I, without water. But it's still damned fine dirt, brung all the way down from the Rockies by the Colorado. It assays out as all sorts of interesting minerals combined. You'll see a few local folk have planted garths as you wander about. Stick a seed in, sprinkle it with water, and step back pronto lest you wind up with a sunflower stalk up your ass."

Stringer said he hadn't come to argue, put down the empty bottle, and asked if he could have a beer. The keeper of local lore chuckled agreeably. "Sure. Order more than one beer and that soda pop was on the house." Then, as he opened a cold beer bottle for Stringer, he observed, "You didn't say what brung you here, if it wasn't to argue about our fine topsoil, stranger."

Stringer nodded and introduced himself. "I'm Stringer MacKail of the *San Francisco Sun*. I came here to look up a gent called Lockwood. Irrigation engineer. I don't suppose you'd know where I could find him?"

The barkeep sighed and said, "You just missed him. Passed you in that hearse, outside. Been dead no more 'n twelve hours. We like to plant 'em pronto out here on the desert."

Stringer accepted the beer but left it untasted for the moment. He whistled softly and replied, "Now that's what I call timing. What did the poor old gent die from?"

The informative barkeep nodded sagely. "Bullets. He wasn't all that old, leastways not from where I stand these days. No more than forty at the most."

Stringer sipped some beer. It wasn't bad, but it wasn't exactly up to Frisco Bay standards either. He tried to keep things casual as he quietly asked, "Does anybody know who murdered him, or why?"

The old-timer replied just as casually, "He wasn't murdered, unless you want to get picky. Lockwood and Cactus Jack Donovan got into an argument over cards, back yonder at the last table as a matter of fact. The shoot-out took place later, out front of course. We don't allow no fighting in here. I didn't see the shoot-out myself. But those who did told the law it seemed a fair enough fight. Cactus Jack rode out anyways. The sheriff had warned him more than once about his nasty disposition."

Stringer sighed and inhaled some more suds. "That's that then. With the man I was sent to see shot and the man who shot him long gone as well, I don't see who on earth my paper might want me to look up here now."

The barkeep thought on this a moment, then offered, "Well, there's that young gal Lockwood was shacked up with if she's still here in town. I wasn't at the funeral, so I just can't say."

Finishing his beer, Stringer thanked him for the suggestion. "I'd best hear what the late Lockwood's play-pretty has to say, as long as I've already come so far on little more than a vague news tip." He pushed back from the bar. "Would you by any chance know where I could find the lady?"

"I never said she was no lady," the barkeep sniffed. "More like a Mex if you ask me. Don't recall her name. But she and Lockwood was camped in a sort of gypsy cart, red wheels, down to the north end of Main Street. You can't miss it. Just look for a red-wheeled cart in the shade of some half-dead cottonwoods."

Stringer paid, leaving his change on the mahogany with a nod of thanks, and strode back out into the blinding sunlight to see how well the old-timer's directions worked.

He could see the treetops down that way and he could also see the old-timer didn't know beans about botany. The trees the old barkeep had described as cottonwoods were really desert willows, which had little more business being this far from a seasonal stream than cottonwoods. But they drooped because they were willows, not because they were dying.

As he ambled along the shady side of the walkless street, a gent riding a dusty roan tore past him, oblivious to the dust he was churning up in the middle of the already dusty enough settlement. Stringer held his breath a good ten paces to let the dust settle back on the street instead of in his lungs, although there wasn't much he could do about the dust in his eyes but blink and bear it.

Stringer had almost forgotten the annoying cuss by the time he passed the last frame shack and its fenced-in garden to spy the gypsy cart parked on four red wheels under the dusty, drooping willow branches. A mule was grazing in a weed patch beyond on a long ground tether. Stringer's amber eyes focused thoughtfully, however, on the lathered pony tethered between him and the gypsy cart. It was the same dusty roan that had passed him just moments before, and Stringer swung around it to make out the source of all the noise coming from near the cart.

The heavy-set, dusty-suited gent who'd abused his horse seemed to be working himself up to abusing a woman now, though so far he was just at the cussing stage. She was a bitty Mex gal, standing her ground on bare feet in a frilly white blouse and a blue circle skirt that exposed a scandalous amount of shapely calf almost to her knees. Stringer had time to note that her face wasn't bad, either.

Neither she nor the burly Anglo fussing with her was aware of Stringer's approach until he was almost upon them. She was facing his way and saw him first but since he looked Anglo as well, she didn't look at all happy to see him.

The rider who'd loped his pony and a whole town dusty to get at her correctly read the way she was staring and turned to give Stringer a once-over. He growled, "Do you have any business here, cowboy?"

Stringer nodded and dropped his gladstone. "Friend of the family. This lady just now buried her *esposo,* if I got the address right. So I'll thank you to simmer down a mite or at least cuss at me intead of her."

The older and bigger man let his dusty frock coat fall open to expose the ivory grips of his cross-draw Colt. "That can be arranged, sonny. I ride for International Irrigation and I've reason to suspect an employee they had to fire rode off with some company papers. All I want from this greaser gal is a look-see inside her wagon. If the papers I'm after are there, I'll just take 'em off her hands. If they ain't, I'll just ride on. I'd say that was fair enough, wouldn't you?"

Stringer smiled thinly and said, "It ain't for me to

say. It's up to this lady here. And don't call her a greaser again. I don't like it."

The girl looked a lot prettier now that she saw she didn't have to shoot daggers from her big sloe eyes at Stringer after all.

"I do not know what this hombre wants," she appealed to Stringer. "I have no papers such as he describes and I will not have my belongings pawed through by rude people I do not know."

Stringer nodded at both of them and told the water company man, "You could both have a point. I'd say your best bet, Amigo, would be a court order. The Constitution gives this little lady the right to total privacy unless and until you can produce a search warrant stating exactly what you're looking for and what business it is of yours to look for the same."

The company rider laughed incredulously. "Are you suffering sun stroke, cowboy? No Mexicans are mentioned in any American constitution."

Stringer shrugged in reply. "In that case you're really out of luck. She wouldn't have to let you search her wagon even if you had a proper search warrant from a California court. Have you considered offering her something for her trouble, or even talking to her respectfully?"

The company rider snorted in disgust. "As a matter of fact I've wasted all the time in talking I ever meant to. I was sent to search for them papers and so now I aim to do so. You'll both stand aside if you know what's good for you."

He put his gun hand casually to his gun grips as a not too subtle hint of his sincerity. Then he found himself staring down the unwinking muzzle of Stringer's .38 as the younger gent he'd taken for a local cowhand with a gallant streak quietly asked, "Why don't you go ahead and tell me just what's good for me?"

The company rider gulped, let go his own gun as if it had just turned into a red-hot poker, and asked, "Have you been mixing the one and original Coca Cola with tequilla, old son? Who said anything here about slapping leather?"

Stringer put his .38 back in its holster. "I'm sure sorry if I misjudged your intent. Where I come from a man doesn't talk growly and pat his gun grips unless he means it. I sure hope we've got that straight. You can see we're both back to scratch now. Go for that hog leg again and I won't be holding my fire. Your move, Amigo."

The company rider kept his gun hand well clear of his far side as he stared thoughtfully at Stringer for a half dozen heart beats. Then he shrugged. "They don't pay me that much. I was told I might have a little trouble from a Mexican spitfire. Nobody mentioned a hired quick-draw artist. So I reckon I'll be leaving now. You wouldn't throw down on a friendly cuss like me as he was mounting up, would you?"

Stringer said, "Depends on how far you keep either hand from that Colt as you do so. Why don't you show me how polite you can ride off, Amigo?"

The company rider did. But as he rode out of easy pistol shot he turned in his saddle and called back, "Maybe next time, Mister Quick Draw!" Then he lit out at full gallop.

Stringer chuckled and said, "Most men hate to back down in front of a woman. I doubt he'll be back without some back-up, ma'am."

Then he saw he was talking to himself. When he turned around, he saw the pretty little gal had climbed up into her cart to rest a shotgun barrel over the bottom wing of the double door built into the rear end under the arched roof. He laughed and told her, "Shucks, ma'am, I thought I was scaring him all by myself."

She smiled back at him, hauling the gun barrel in, as she told him, "I think you made a believer of him the first time you displayed your lightning draw, señor. I am called Juanita Vasques, by the way. Were you a friend of poor Herberto?"

Stringer moved closer, saying, "Never met him. He sent a news tip to my paper, the *San Francisco Sun*. They sent me down here to talk to him. My name would be, ah, Stuarto MacKail, señora."

She corrected him. "That would be señorita, por favor. I do not understand why everyone seems to think I was married to poor Herberto Lockwood. He was simply living with me in this *carreta*. Where is your own mount, Stuarto?"

He stared up at her, bemused, as he sorted out what she'd just said. "I don't have one. I just got here by train."

"In that case you had better find a pony for to ride far and fast," she advised him earnestly. "That malo will be back with others, if I know the people he works for. I shall hitch up my mule as you go over to the livery near the railroad stop for to hire a good Spanish riding mule, not a pony, for our escape, no?"

He smiled incredulously and said, "Hold on, Juanita. I only came to have a few words with you, not to join you in a war with that water outfit."

She opened the bottom of the Dutch door to drop lightly to the ground beside him. "We shall have plenty of time for to talk, once we are a safe distance from here. You do not have to declare war on International Irrigation. They declare war on you if they feel you are in their way. And, just now, we both got in their way.

You can come with me or you can catch the next train out. If you stay here, they will kill you, comprendo?"

"I do now," Stringer assured her. "I'll be back with a mount directly. I've yet to get a good story by running away from it."

CHAPTER
FIVE

The Spanish riding mule was bigger, stronger, and almost as fast as most cow ponies. The real advantage of any mule in dry country was that it got by on less than half the water a horse needed. So while vaqueros felt almost as dumb aboard a mule as a gringo buckaroo, they'd bred a pretty good mount with the size and gait of its usually Arab mamma and the toughness and stolid ways of its burro daddy. The sterile jenny Stringer picked up at the livery cost him thirty dollars and change, with a beat-up but serviceable bare-tree Mexican saddle and horsehair bridle thrown in for another ten. They'd flatly refused to hire him by the day once he'd mentioned he might be riding out on the desert. He knew Juanita had the shotgun aboard her gypsy cart. But as long as he was in downtown El Centro and meant to let the *Sun* pay these unforeseen travel expenses, if they would, he picked up a used Winchester and a couple of boxes of .44-.40 and some more .38 Longs at the hardware store next door.

He was halfway back to the willows when he met up with Juanita in her cart, coming toward him. As he wheeled his mule to fall in beside her, she called, "I put your bag in the back. I did not open it."

"I never thought you would," he assured her. Then he asked, "How come we're headed north? I thought Old Mexico was the other way."

She seemed to repress a shudder as she replied, "I would rather take my chances with hired gringo guns than Los Indios in the desert to the south."

He asked, "How many wild Indians do you still have down Mexico way?"

"Too many," she replied. "Those hiding from the Federáles in the bleakest parts of the desert are most desperate. They do not attack because they hate your kind and mine. They attack anything that moves because if it moves they feel free to eat it or rob it."

Stringer figured she knew what she was doing, and he followed her lead without more questions. When they had crossed the railroad tracks and began pushing through greasewood, she sighed and explained further. "Herberto and I came to El Centro for to be above the floodwaters when they swept in from the east. I do not know how far north we can go before we are lower than the Sea of Cortez. But we must go somewhere and Herberto said any ground higher than the beaches of long ago should be high enough."

Stringer swept their seemingly dead-flat surroundings with his eyes. There was nothing in the way of a serious dip or rise before the purple mountains in the east and west looming above the horizon. There was nothing above the horizon line to the north or south.

"If this is what Lockwood called high ground," he commented, "I can't wait to see what he called low ground. It looks mighty flat to me."

She nodded in reply. "That is for why Herberto was a water engineer and you and I are not. Did you see those trees back there, where first we met? Herberto said they had sprouted there and grown so fast because all the well water that people threw out as slops ran north, but, of course, mucho slowly. Herberto said that long before Cortez or even Cristo the sea reached as far inland as the town of Indio, far to the north, almost a hundred of your Yanqui miles. Do not ask me for why this is all very dry ground today. When we make camp I can show you the charts he drew. I do not understand them. Pero, that hombre who came for them may have. That is for why I did not want to give them to him. I do not think it was fair of them to fire Herberto for being wrong if they thought he was right, do you?"

Stringer shook his head and turned in the saddle to gaze back the way they'd just come. The rooftops of El Centro weren't half as far back as he'd hoped they'd be by now, and in the shimmering heat waves he just couldn't tell whether anyone back there was showing any interest in their departure or not.

He told the girl, "Keep driving. I'm fixing to rein in here for a spell to cover our retreat."

When she asked if anyone was following them, he said that was what he meant to find out. She nodded and drove on, while Stringer drew the Winchester from its saddle boot and dismounted to rest his mule. As long as he had the chance, he decided to water some grease-wood, keeping his back well turned to the onward-moving cart. If anyone to the south was close enough to see his fool pecker, they were way too close.

While his mule nibbled experimentally on some salt bush that was struggling to grow amid the greasewood, Stringer cradled the saddle gun with one elbow and rolled a smoke. A black dot that could have been a mounted rider, or most anything else, kept bouncing back and forth in the shimmering air but didn't seem to be getting any closer by the time Stringer had finished his smoke. He turned to see how Juanita was making out. He swore softly when he saw the gypsy cart looked no farther away and only a mite smaller than it had the last time he'd looked. He calculated rapidly in his head and muttered to himself. "Let's see. The horizon's about three miles off to a rider in the saddle. That cart's moving less than three miles an hour. Rooftops stick up above the horizon. So that makes it another two or three hours minimum before we can even consider a serious stop." He glanced up at the sun and saw it was a little over halfway down in the west from its zenith. "Ought to be safe to trailbreak before snake time."

Then he rolled another smoke. He'd been born too late for the real Indian fighting in the west. But the war with Spain had taught him a thing or two about patience. Nine out of ten times a man was just wasting his time covering the back trail. But that tenth time could leave him feeling dead as well as foolish. He didn't know which way that water company rider had gone after crawfishing out of sight. There hadn't been a train through El Centro since then, and even if there had been the gent had been mounted. That meant he had to have ridden cross-country to wherever the gents he worked for might be. Of course, he might have stayed in town to sulk or mayhaps wire home for help. If he'd been sipping Coca Cola in any saloon along Main Street, he'd have had to notice them leaving. But, wherever he was, the company man didn't seem to be trailing Juanita's now fairly distant cart.

Stringer turned to study the wagon ruts that had been left when the cart moved on. He was pleased to see they were not as clear as he'd feared. He was more used to

the Mojave and other western deserts, where the topsoil
was covered by a more brittle crust of so-called "desert
pavement." Busting through caliche left ruts that lasted
until at least one hell of a rain storm. And in desert
country it seldom rained. But this odd soil didn't have a
crust worth mentioning. So, while the wheels sank in
deep enough, their impressions weren't sharp, and the
gentle ground breezes were already starting to fill the
ruts with drifting baby-powder silt. Small wonder then,
he mused, that he hadn't seen any other tracks out here
so close to a town.

He filled his hat with canteen water and fed it to the
mule. Then he allowed himself a few gulps and put the
wet hat back on. It sure felt good as the rapid evapora-
tion of the desert cooled his head. He was tempted to
mount up and ride on while he still felt up to it, but he
rolled another smoke instead. By the time he'd smoked
that one down, the gypsy cart was just another wavering
dot in the shimmering distance.

"Well," Stringer told his patient mule, "if he don't
want a fight, he don't want a fight." So he remounted
and set after Juanita at a walk, knowing his riding mule
walked faster than the poor brute pulling the gypsy cart.

It still took quite a while to catch up, and by the time
he reached her Juanita looked as if she'd been crying.

"I was so worried, Stuarto!" she cried. "What kept
you so long back there?"

He said reassuringly. "Nothing. But I had to stay put
long enough to make sure. I could tell you a tale of
Spanish cavalry raiders surprising the daylights out of a
supply train down in Cuba one time. But it wouldn't be
polite to tell such war stories to a Spanish lady. Let's
just say I'm a quick learner."

She smiled at him. "Thank you for calling me Spanish as well as a lady. My father had some Spanish

blood, it is true. Pero, my mother was almost pure Pima."

He nodded soberly and declared, "That makes you half-Americano, then. The Pima scouted for the U.S. Cavalry during the Apache wars on this side of the border."

"I do not know for myself," she replied. "Mamacita did not like to discuss that side of her family. My father was a Mexican trader. It was from him I inherited this cart. My brother and me, we brought a load of mescal up from Sonora for to sell to the workers along the big water canal to the east. My brother was shot by a mean gringo for some reason. It was about then the water company fired Herberto and so . . ."

"That's none of my business," Stringer cut in. But then he added, "When we have the chance I'd surely like to go over those mysterious papers his former employers seem so interested in. Whether he left wedding certificates among his effects or not is none of my beeswax."

She frowned hard at the rump of the mule ahead of her. Then she asked, "Wedding what? Did you think Herberto and me were man and wife, Stuarto?"

He said, "I'm not paid to think about such matters. I don't do the social pages for the *Sun*. But as long as we're on the subject of the poor cuss, are you up to telling me about that gunfight he lost with Cactus Jack Donovan the other night?"

She sighed. "I only know what they told me later. I was surprised for to hear poor Herberto got in a fight with a notorious malo, or anyone else. He was a most gentle person, even drunk."

"Oh, did he drink a lot?" asked Stringer.

"Si," she replied. "He was most upset about losing his job and even more worried about the big flood he kept warning everyone about. It made him angry when

they all laughed at him and said it was most foolish to
worry about high water where water is so rare. *Pero*, he
never got angry enough to fight with anyone. To tell the
truth, I do not think he knew how to fight. I know he
did not wear a gun like you. Don't you find it strange
that a man so mild would wish for to fight a famous
gunfighter?"

Stringer frowned thoughtfully and replied, "It might
not have been his notion. Could this Cactus Jack by any
chance happen to be on the payroll of International Irrigation?"

She answered, *"Quien sabe?* He is, as I said, what
my people call a *malo*, a bad one. Some say his gun
hand is for hire, while others say he is simply evil-tem-
pered. For why do you find this important, Stuarto?
Herberto is dead, no matter why he was shot down in
the streets of El Centro, no?"

Stringer growled, "I'm not dead, yet, and I find it
mighty odd that someone tried to gun me, about the
same time, miles away from a less fortunate gent who
might have had something he wanted to tell me. I wish I
had a better notion what it might have been. To tell the
truth, we get lots of crank letters and hardly any of 'em
pan out as news worth printing. So mayhaps old Herb
was more than a disgruntled employee with odd notions
after all. Hardly anyone shoots pure cranks, let alone
innocent reporters on their way to listen to pure jabber."

She demanded further explanation. So he filled her in
on his misadventures in L. A., leaving out any mention
of Zelda, who'd no doubt by this time rejoined her husband in San Diego feeling a mite smug about the fun
she'd had and the traveling expenses she'd saved on her
most recent trip to and from her sister.

The pretty gal closer to hand and certainly not married took a dimmer view of her own people than

Stringer. She said she was of the opinion one of those Chicano kids had tailed him to his hotel and gone home for a rifle.

Stringer said, "That works fine, I'll allow. So does a fired and somewhat drunken engineer blundering into a shoot-out with yet another surly pest. But when you add both incidents up, you get a coincidence even Jack London would hesitate to use in one of his wild Alaska yarns."

She said she didn't know what "coincidence" meant. So he told her, "Try *fortuna ciego*. What are the odds on two men who'd never met, but were fated to meet, getting shot at about the same time by pure accident?"

She nodded gravely. "Perhaps the two happenings were only meant to look like unrelated trouble by someone who did not wish for the two of you to ever meet. Pero, Stuarto, if that was the case for why would they wish for to kill both of you? Would not the death of one of you alone serve as well to prevent you from ever meeting?"

He said, "They may have sent someone after both of us to make sure one or the other died. I wouldn't be here talking about it if I hadn't proven it's possible to miss. I wish I knew as much about them as they seem to know about me. You see, once a good newshound gets the scent he's inclined to keep sniffing until he finds something out. They didn't bother you about any papers old Herb might have left with you until they'd had time to find out I was still alive. I suspect they wanted to make sure I never laid eyes on 'em. So how far out here were you planning to roll before the first trail break? I'd sure like to see what your man might have left in the back of this cart."

She reined in her draft mule immediately. "Our beasts could use a rest. I will show you the papers right now." So, as Stringer dismounted and tethered his mule to one clump of scrub, Juanita dropped down off her seat to tether the other. Both animals had to be watered before they did anything else, but that only took a moment. Then she led him around to the back of the cart, and they both climbed into the stuffy interior. The heat inside was oppressive, but it took only one sniff to tell that Juanita was a mighty clean housekeeper. The sun beating down all day on the canvas roof had baked the scent of lemon oil and pine soap out of the paneling and spartan furnishings. There was a hint of chili pepper and toilet water in the air as well, but not a whiff of bedbug or chamber pot. He saw two bunk beds folded up against one side, while the other was lined with chests that no doubt served both for seating and as tabletops. One chest was an old army footlocker. Juanita dropped to her knees to open it, lifting out the top tray filled with men's shaving gear, clean socks, and a brass barometer. Then she handed him a sheaf of papers, neatly bound with a rubber band. "I think these are what that company rider must have been after. Herberto had nothing else of value here. Such money as he had would have been on him when he was killed. I did not ask about it. So perhaps they saw no need to mention it to me."

Stringer grimaced and said he knew about small-town undertaking customs. Then he found a seat on another chest and opened what looked like a survey map.

It was. In fact it appeared to be a printed government survey map of the so-called Imperial Valley and hence mostly blank. He found pencil lines on it as well that nobody but the late Herbert Lockwood had likely felt called to draw in, neatly but lightly, with hard lead. Stringer knew engineers in the interest of accuracy liked to draw lines too skinny for anyone but a spider to notice. Once he got used to the contrast between the printed ink lines and the spiderweb of faint penciling, he was able to read the survey map fairly well. But it failed to explain why anyone would have wanted the man who drew them all that dead.

The canal lines Lockwood had drawn from a point just below Yuma didn't seem to be leading water, if they were leading any water at all, more alarmingly than Sam Barca had mentioned back in the pressroom in Frisco. It was easy to see that the neat little dashes across the original main channel dug by Chaffey meant the channel was blocked—or perhaps each dash indicated the channel had been cleaned out to that point. The newer southern channel, parts of it looping south of the Mexican border as it aimed for the desert crossing of Calexico-Mexicali, and a fossil streambed leading south to the sea had symbols here and there that might have indicated floodgates. Dotted lines ran north from each, which Stringer assumed indicated canals to be dug at some future date. To the north, cutting across the tops of the more complex and even skinnier lines of the irrigation maze, ran the diversion canal that was intended to get temporary water to the area while the original silted-up canal was being cleaned out to do the job properly. Since the Southern Pacific had crossed the same desert a lot earlier, its railbed was printed in ink. Stringer had to peer hard to distinguish the diversion canal that was being dug in line with it. The water scheme made more sense once he saw that, although the new canal was being run south of the tracks and crossed feeder ditches that apparently ran under the railroad through culverts. Barca had been right apparently about the Southern Pacific working in cahoots with the water outfit. But Stringer failed to see anything more criminal than the idea sounded in the first place. So where was the news? News was stuff that had happened recently. The half-baked plans of old Charly Rockwood had been third page news at least three or more years back.

Stringer almost missed the spidery handwritten notations the late Herb Lockwood had added in an even lighter hand, as if meant for his own eyes alone. There was naturally a surveyed contour line around the whole so-called valley, marked, "Mean Sea Level." Out in the middle of what had once been a vast shallow lagoon lay Salton's Sink, the deepest part, had there still been a drop of water within miles of its thirsty salt flats. The survey bench marks indicated Salton's Sink lay a good fifty feet or more below the level of the Gulf of Mexico, many miles to the south. That was not as ominous as Lockwood's penciled-in notation reading, "Wrong! At least minus 300 feet!"

Stringer whistled thoughtfully. But even if the dead engineer was right, Salton's Sink was still a hell of a ways out on bone-dry desert floor. Nobody was ever going to settle on land half that salty, and if the sink was that deep, it figured to take one hell of a lot more water to its salty bosom than anyone would ever be able to drain into it through mere irrigation ditches. The problem on land this flat, or land with such a gentle grade at least, would be getting the water to run anywhere, as it had to eventually lest it salt the irrigated farmland. The Colorado was a semi-saline stream to begin with, and nobody had been joshing when they'd named one of the Gila's main tributaries the Salt River.

Stringer held the map slantwise to the light to make sure he hadn't missed anything. He saw he had. Smack across the route of the temporary diversion canal to the north, Lockwood had impatiently scrawled, "Remember the Alamo!"

Stringer lowered the penciled-over chart to his knees to think about that. At first reading it had struck him

that poor old Herb had been out in the sun too long. For
the Alamo was one hell of a ways off in space and time
combined. The Mexican border was a lot closer, of
course. Could the dead man have meant an attack by
mad Mexican ditch diggers?

Stringer muttered aloud. "That's just too cock-eyed
to consider. Even if some Mexicans were plotting
against the gringo water lords, they'd hit first at the
south canal, parts of it inside Mexico, for heaven's
sake."

He recalled from the morgue material Barca had
given him to read on the train that as either the California or Imperial Valley holding company, old Rockwood
had negotiated a deal with El Presidente Diaz to dig up
parts of otherwise useless Mexican desert. Nobody else
was allowed to plot anything all that important down
Mexico way these days. Lockwood's hasty warning
made no sense. So why had the subcontractors he'd
been working for fired him and then had him killed once
they'd found out he'd made off with these very charts?

Stringer and Juanita resumed their journey, across
what appeared to be dead-level desert. But when they
stopped just before sunset to make camp before snake
time Stringer was not surprised to discover Lockwood's
barometer now said they were a few feet lower. Or else
it was going to rain like hell in a little while, despite the
cloudless cobalt blue bowl above them.

"I can see why old Herb had some trouble convinc-
ing others," Stringer told Juanita. "It takes scientific in-
struments to make out any slope at all out here, and it
could still just mean some rain at this time of the year.
The winter months are the only time it ever rains, and
even then it never rains much."

She put the coffee on the coals and huddled closer to
him. "Herberto said they had their own ways of measur-

ing such things. Pero, they chose not to . . . how you say, check, when he warned them they were running the new canal too far to the north of what he called a divide. Does that make any sense to you?"

Stringer grimaced. "It sure does! I'm no hydraulic engineer. But I've slopped over a bathtub or two in my time, and no matter how flat the tile floor ever looked the water always wound up in one corner or another. It hardly takes a college education to see you wouldn't want more than a fraction of the Colorado River draining inland rather than the other way. I wish I had a map of the Southern Pacific's land grants with some bench marks giving the altitudes."

Although she asked why, in a sleepy voice, he knew she had to be less interested than he was. Still, he answered. "It's been my experience that big shots only act dumb as hell when there's money to be made out of sheer stupidity. If they fired Lockwood for stating the simple truth, they must not have wanted to hear the truth. I'll likely never be an empire-builder. I guess I was stuck at birth with the considerable handicap of a conscience. But if I was a money hungry son of a never-mind and I had a whole mess of land to sell that couldn't be irrigated as simply as I was offering to do so, I might just ignore things like the laws of nature and go on and peddle gold bricks and promises as long as I could."

She yawned again and apologized. "Forgive me, I am too sleepy for to make fresh tortillas tonight. Would you mind very much if we just had cold beans and coffee, Stuarto?"

He said he was sleepy too and agreed beans would be more than enough. He opened the can for her while she rustled up some tin cups and saucers. As they lazed by the dying fire after their modest repast, enjoying the cool breezes that sprang up after dark, he began to wonder whether coffee had been such a grand notion after all. It was early evening for him, but sleeping seemed to be the only entertainment the desert had to offer after sundown. Juanita must have felt some effects from her own two cups of strong black coffee, for again she asked him, "Perhaps you would like to know about Herberto and me, no?"

He grimaced and said, "No. I said it was no business of mine and I meant it."

She nodded. "I thought that was what made you feel so hesitant. Is it not the usual custom for a princess to reward the gallant caballero who saves her from the dragon with at least one little kiss?"

He laughed at the picture despite himself and said, "He wasn't much of a dragon. But what did old Herb save you from, Juanita?"

She shrugged. "It was I who saved him. He had been simpatico to my brother before my brother was killed. When the same cruel ones who murdered my poor brother threw poor Herberto out of their work camp to find his way out of the desert on his own, I felt obliged for to take him in. As you may have noticed, there are two beds inside my *carreta*. I know you find this hard to believe—pero, I hope you do not think I was sleeping with my own brother before he was killed!"

Stringer shook his head politely but had to ask, "How far did you have to haul the late Herbert Lock-wood from that work camp and how come he was still living with you once you made it back to civilization if he was just . . . whatever he was to you."

She said simply, "He was my friend. He said he had to wait in El Centro for someone who might pay him much money for something. I think he meant you. I told him I did not need his money as long as he helped around camp and bought his own liquor. I was made most sad when Cactus Jack shot him. I liked him, as one may like a friendly old *gato* with nobody else to take him in. But he was no more than that to me. I am most particular about men I may make love with."

Stringer didn't need to be hit over the head with a ton of bricks and it would have been cruel to make the sweet little gal hint more broadly. So he just hauled her in for a howdy kiss. Then he asked her if he might be the sort of gent she had in mind.

She held him tightly and murmured, *"Es verdad*. But not out here in front of the mules. Let us make love inside, no?"

Stringer had long since learned it was the nature of women to lie to him at least as much as he lied to them. But long before midnight Juanita had convinced him that if her relationship with old Herb Lockwood had been anything but platonic the poor sap hadn't been treating her right.

Juanita was a natural enthusiast with simple tastes in good old-fashioned loving. The narrow bottom bunk precluded really wild positions, but happily she didn't need exotic postures to stay hot. In fact she stayed so hot that Stringer needed little in the way of added inspiration, and they simply kept going at it like healthy hard-up kids who'd just found out why boys and girls were built so different. Juanita's tawny young body was about as different from Zelda's as it could get and still be sexually utile. She got a charge out of the way he could cup her firm little buttocks in his palms while she rubbed her nose like an Eskimo in his chest hair. Her turgid nipples felt odd but nice as far down his torso as she kept sliding them back and forth. But since all good things must come to an end, usually sooner than bad things, there came a time when they just had to stop.

Being as the bunk was so narrow, Stringer had to sit on the edge of it as he groped for his shirt and the makings while she just lay there, crooning Spanish love words and assuring him he was the first man who'd ever made her climax that many times in a row.

He'd just found his tobacco pouch and matches when they both heard little wet frogs hopping about on the canvas above them. She laughed and said, *"Carramba! That sounds like rain!"*

He replied, "I noticed. It has to rain everywhere now and again, and this is the season for such rain as this desert ever gets."

He struck a match to have a look at the barometer hanging in the center of the enclosure. She sighed and said, "Madre de Dios you have a most manly body, querido!" To which he replied with a fond chuckle, "I'd never take your sweet shape for a man's by sun or shadow."

Stinger peered at the barometer. "The needle's at 30.04 now. I don't see how this cart could have sunk that deep in the dirt since we stopped here. So I reckon the extra pressure is due to the weather outside." Then he shook out the match to roll a smoke in the dark as he listened to the rain drumming on the canvas. "I'm sure glad we're inside. It figures to rain harder before it rains lighter. Anyone who's been dogging our hoof and wagon sign is welcome to get chilled to the bone, camped out among the soggy greasewood."

She asked, "Do you not think this rain will wipe out our trail by morning if it keeps up?" But before he could agree the rain might at least blur it, the sky above split open with a mighty crack of lightning, which they saw even through the wet canvas roof, and then it began to rain in earnest. Raising his voice above the drumming on the hopefully waterproof canvas, he said, "Yep. I'd say you could consider us lost in the desert."

He finished rolling and sealing his smoke. As he lit it, he saw she was propped up on one elbow, looking somewhat confused as well as surprisingly tempting to a man who'd just rolled off her. He said, "I didn't mean we were lost, personal. I meant I doubt anyone but mayhaps a Digger Indian could read any trail we left betwixt here and El Centro, and I doubt we have any Indians after us."

She said, "Bueno. Pero, where do we go from here now that we have escaped those bad hombres who want poor Herberto's papers?"

It was a good question, and he wasn't sure he had a good answer. "Well, I seem to have such a story as old Herb wanted to tell us, but I doubt my paper will run it on any front page."

"The people he was working for seemed to think it was important enough. Why did they get so rough with all of us if you think there is nothing to it, Stuarto?"

He blew smoke out his nostrils with a bare-shouldered shrug of annoyance. "Guilty consciences, I reckon. Hired guns don't know half as much about running a newspaper as we do. To them, the fact they're slickering settlers with an irrigation scheme that might not work, assuming I could prove that, must sound like the makings of a headline exposé. They just don't know how cramped a newspaper is for space to print more solid news. I'll type what I've found out once I get back to my old grasshopper. I may even get paid space rates for it. But if they run the few padded paragraphs I can manage at all, it'll be as a filler on a back page. It's simply not fresh news that slickers have been selling worthless western land to suckers since Jefferson beat down the price of the Louisiana Purchase."

She protested. "Pero, Herberto said it was a most

important tale to be told. He said the water company was tampering with nature and that there was going to be great flood for to rival the one in the Bible."

Stringer inhaled another drag and let it out thoughtfully. "It would still take a heap of water and a heap of time to fill that natural basin Lockwood thinks he surveyed on his own. Nobody lives out in the heart of this desert. So how much damage could it do? A big fresh water lake betwixt here and Indio might be an improvement on all this dusty nothing-much, right?"

Then he blew some more smoke out and mused aloud. "Hold on. It wouldn't wind up a fresh water lake. It would pick up the salt from that dried-up earlier sea and. . . . All right, so we'd have California's answer to the Great Salt Lake, only bigger. That would be worth a Sunday feature, if I knew for sure such a thing was ever sure to happen. But I've no way to prove it. The land and water mongers would be sure to deny it. It's not a story worth the risk of a libel suite either way."

She lay back yawning and asked how soon he meant to return to the pet grasshopper he seemed so fond of. He laughed and explained. "I call my second-hand Remington typewriter a grasshopper. You'd have to see the way the roll bounces when I push the upper-case shift to understand the nickname. And I'm not that fond of it. It just pays a lot better than working cows. As to when I have to get back to it, I'm not in any great hurry if you have something more interesting in mind."

She giggled and said, "I'm a little tired, right now. Pero, I do not have to head back to Sonora just yet. Do you think we could get tired of one another in a month or so?"

He was sure they could. That was why they called the first month of even a serious relationship the honeymoon. But he knew she didn't want to hear that. Instead he said, "Well, if you have the time I have the nerve. This is the best time of the year for exploring the desert and I'd like to see just how serious one ought to take old Lockwood's disaster warnings. The salt flats of that seldom-visited Salton's Sink can't be more than twenty to thirty miles to the north—a day each way by cartwheel. Why don't we talk about what happens next after we have us a look at all that salt?"

She thought it was such a grand notion that by the time he put out the last of his smoke she was ready to haul him down and wrap her sweet limbs around him again. He didn't mind. Few men would have. The rain drumming on the canvas above them seemed to inspire them both to a new tempo. But she finally got where she wanted to go and went limp under him while he caught up with her. She protested that she was sleepy and that he'd taken advantage of her weak nature, so he stopped, saying, "I'd best spread some tarps to take advantage of all this free water."

Being a woman, she hugged him tighter and insisted they had all the water they needed in the kegs lashed to the chassis outside. So he lay still and just held her, as he knew she wanted to be held, until her soft breathing told him she was asleep. Then he gently rolled off the narrow mattress, covered her with a quilt and, seeing they might not have to worry about water after all, climbed up in the top bunk to stretch out and close his eyes.

CHAPTER
SIX

The next thing Stringer knew it was morning. Some desert quail were bitching about it outside, and he seemed to be alone in Juanita's gypsy cart. So he swung down to the floor planks, wiped the sleep gum out of his eyes, and hauled on his boots, jeans, and .38 rig to see what was going on out there.

The rain had stopped. But the sky above was overcast, and the air felt more like spring in greener country than the way it usually felt out here.

He walked around the cart to find Juanita, naked as a jaybird, hunkered on her bare heels over the greasewood fire she was kindling. She looked more like a naked Spanish lady than the Digger Indian she seemed to be play-acting this morning. He chuckled and told her so. She shrugged and asked, "Who is there to peek out here who has not seen me, and more, in this costume? For why did you put your pants on, querido? Are you ashamed to let me see what feels so good in the dark?"

He said, "I'd look mighty dumb in just my boots,

and I'm not about to walk through sticker brush bare-
footed. I'm going to backtrack us a ways as soon as I
water and nose-bag the mules."

She shook her head and said, "I watered and fed
them at dawn, you most sleepy but handsome *perezoso*.
Don't go too far. I mean to feed you as soon as I can get
this wet wood to behave."

He nodded and strode back the way they'd come the
previous day. He knew she'd get the greasewood to
burn. That was why they called it greasewood. The stuff
wasn't good for much else. It grew slow, twisty, and
impregnated with waxy resin. The rain they'd just had
would make all the brush he could see for miles sprout
perhaps a fraction of an inch. Each greasewood clump
was surrounded by a few feet of bare soil. The tough,
thirsty bushes hoarded all the water that fell anywhere
near them by poisoning the surrounding soil with a toxin
given off by their roots. It made for easy passage between the prickly stuff, and it was here that he scouted
for sign.

There wasn't much now, thanks to that heavy rain.
But here and there he could just make out a puddle that
might have formed in a soft spot a wagon wheel or hoof
had dug into. The puddles were almost gone now, despite the overcast sky and unusually moist air. He spotted a big one, formed naturally where wind had scoured
the dust on the lee side of a brush clump. He hunkered
down and drew a line in the damp dirt with his finger.
The water in the puddle didn't seem interested in running south. He tried a tiny ditch to the north. The water
filled it as fast as he could move his finger through the
dirt. He nodded and muttered aloud, "All right, Herb.
You were right. I doubt we could be below sea level,
therefore we have to be north of an almost dead-flat

divide. So, no water on this side has any outlet to the sea."

He straightend up, wiping the damp grit from his finger on his jeans, and headed back to rejoin Juanita as he stared due north at what seemed to be dead-flat desolation. There were no signs of erosion, however. Rainwater soaked into the thirsty silt too fast to run enough to matter in any direction. He found Juanita frying bacon in a cast-iron spider. He hunkered down beside her and announced, "I dunno. If they hadn't shot old Herb, I'd feel more sure he was just a worrywart. If they're running a mite north of such north-south drainage as there is, north-bound irrigation water ought to just soak in before it can cause any damage. Maybe I'd better have a look at his other charts and see if I can make heads or tails of his fuss with the water company."

She told him he wasn't going anywhere without a proper breakfast. So he stayed put, wondering idly just how long it was apt to take before she got down to the serious nagging that tended to dry the dew from the rose and remind a man of all the thorns that went with such delights. But when she suggested sex al fresco for dessert he decided she hadn't meant to sound so bossy after all.

They were just starting to climax together when a gentle rain swept across the desert floor to inspire them to try again and left them laughing, feeling clean but a mite chilled. So they got dressed, broke camp, and continued to move north through alternate spells of soft rain and bright but not too hot sunshine. Even the mules seemed to enjoy such unusually decent desert weather. So they made good time until Stringer, scouting out ahead, reined in and raised his free hand to halt Juanita and her cart. As he rode back to her he said, "I want to have another peek at that barometer. It looks as if we've come to a sort of fossil beach."

She climbed down and moved forward to see what he was talking about while he dismounted and climbed up into the back of her cart.

The needle on Herb Lockwood's barometer read 29.98, or a tad below or above mean sea level, depending on the weather. He climbed back out and walked over to join Juanita. He found her holding a bitty prehistoric conch shell to her ear. She smiled at him and cried, "I hear it. I can hear the sea, inside, just like they say!"

He stared curiously around, replying, "Any sea that ever made a sound around here is long gone, indeed." Certainly there was no actual beach to be seen cutting east and west across their path. The desert winds and rains had long since done away with any traces of wave action and the knee-high, slate-gray greasewood had marched right out into what must have been a very shallow sea in its time. The old waterline was there to be seen only because of the sun-bleached seashells spread out across the bare silt. Stringer was no expert on the topic, but most of the shells seemed to be those of salt-water mussels. The conch shell Juanita had found just didn't go with fresh water. So, all right, there'd been a time when anyone standing here would have been staring across open blue water to the north horizon, with the vast inland sea cradled between the bare brown mountains, east and west, perhaps thirty to fifty miles apart. He started to turn back to Juanita. Then he spotted a chalky conch shell bigger than the one she'd found, and he bent to pick it up for her.

The son of a bitch drawing a rifle bead on Stringer must not have expected him to duck like that. His .30-.30 round buzzed right through the air Stringer's

back had just been filling. Stringer did a forward somer-
sault as the rifle squibbed again, winding up prone in a
clump of greasewood with his own gun drawn. He spit
out curses and pungent twigs while he tried to figure out
what in thunder was going on.

He lifted his hat on his six-gun barrel. But the unseen
marksman didn't fall for that. So he tried sticking his
bare head up a few feet and almost got it blown off. He
ducked at the sight of the muzzle flash before the sound
and the bullet could cover the quarter mile between
them. The bastard was good, Stringer decided. This was
going to take some study. He started by crawling toward
the gypsy cart and his Winchester, grateful that the recent rain had made the ground less dusty and trying to
think like a lizard as he slithered through the knee-high
brush, being careful not to move any of it. He heard
another shot. It sounded as if the cuss was lobbing
rounds into his old position for luck. He'd left his hat
atop a bush back there. The bastard might be good but
he sure was stupid, Stringer thought—nobody with a
lick of sense would have put a light gray hat back on at
a time like this.

The rear of the cart, Dutch door and all, was exposed
to the sneaky bastard who'd cut their trail. He'd have to
get into the wagon from the driver's seat. Juanita's mule
was tethered between the poles, and it showed him the
white of one eye as he slithered out of the shrubbery
toward the animal with a reassuring whisper. Fortunately, Juanita had tied it to a stout clump, so it had to
just stay put, kicking its big hooves more in uncertainty
than lethal intent as Stringer crawled under it. Nevertheless, Stringer took a couple of half-hearted kicks before
he could get to the wagon and haul himself up over the
dashboard to roll over Juanita's seat to the inside.

He scooped up his Winchester, levered a round in the

chamber, and eased back to the rear door. He opened the bottom half just a crack and spotted two Spanish mules half a mile out. He had to stand and crack the top door before he could make out the two hats just visible above the slate-blue brush. His attackers were both hunkered smart from the point of view of anyone at ground level, but in the cart he was standing a good yard higher. One hat was Anglo, a peaked Arizona rider. The other was a more Mex sombrero. Even as he watched, both were moving in, spread about ten yards apart. He took a bead on the Anglo farthest away. Then he fired and levered his weapon to fire again as the one in the Mex hat made the mistake of rising to fire back at him. The other rifleman's bullet thunked into the doorjamb near Stringer's head. But from the way that sombrero went skyward, Stringer knew he'd aimed better. Heads seldom jerked that hard unless a gent had been spine-shot.

That left the Anglo he'd first fired at, who was hit or playing possum but in either case out of sight. So Stringer swung the door wide open and dropped out and down. The rifle round that whizzed over the cart told him the bastard was still in business out there.

Stringer started crawling again, with the Winchester cradled across his forearms. Had not it been for a similar incident down Cuba way one time, Stringer might have tried crawling in on the bastard's last known position. But he didn't. He'd learned as a war correspondent who hadn't expected to fight but then had to, that one-third to fifty percent casualties inspired most men to retreat, and the average bushwacker wasn't as brave as most men. So Stringer made for the mules he'd spotted tethered farther out.

It worked. When the man he'd shot out from under the Arizona hat figured he'd crawled far enough with a

.44-40 slug in his left shoulder and got up to make the last dash for his mule and other parts, Stringer rose between him and said mules to snap, "Freeze!" And, when that didn't work, he nailed the cuss again at closer range.

Stringer bulled through the brush to where he'd dropped his man, lest the son of a bitch have time to recover some spunk if he was still alive. But he wasn't. He was just spawled there with a kind of smile on his ugly face and what looked like blueberry jam all over the front of his black shirt.

Stringer shot him again to make sure. The muzzle blast set the black sateen to smouldering, but Stringer didn't care. He hunkered down to go through the dead man's pockets. He wound up with forty-three dollars and one of those mail-order private detective buzzers that went with company dicks. A wilted card assured anyone who might have cared that the rascal had been a water outfit security man called Wordsworth. Stringer got to his feet, putting the money away, and muttered, "I didn't think much of your namesake's poetry either." Then he went looking for the Mex he'd downed.

As he approached the fossil beach once more he called out to Juanita, "It's over, honey. I got the rascals." There was no answer. She'd likely started running when she'd heard that first rifleshot, he decided. He just hoped she hadn't run too far.

It took him some minutes to find the dead Mex and, when he did, the dead face staring up at him looked more Indian. He nodded and told the moon-faced cadaver, "I didn't think we'd left enough sign for your average white man to follow."

There was no identification on the dead Indian. Stringer took charge of the twenty-dollar double eagle and silver quarter he'd found on that one and headed back to the cart, calling out to Juanita some more.

He finally found her not far from where he'd last seen her, lying on her back with the fossil seashell still in one hand. She looked as if she was sleeping, but he didn't try to wake her up. There was a little blue hole in her forehead and a thread of blood had run out her ear, soaking into the shiny black hair spread all around her pretty face like a perverse halo.

Stringer walked back to the cart and slammed his free fist into the side of it, hard. It didn't help. He dropped his rifle and clung to one of the red wheels, puking up the breakfast she'd just served him along with her sweet little self. Then he got control of himself again and rummaged in the tool box under the wagon bed to break out a short-handled spade.

He buried the sweet, harmless little gal on the fossil shore of the ghost sea, wrapped in a tarp with the pretty shell she'd admired clasped in her dead hands. Stringer wasn't much on religion. But as he smoothed the last soft silt over her he took off his hat to murmur, *"Vaya con Dios, querida. I sure hope that there's a heaven and that they'll take you in. You have my word that if there's a hell I mean to send the sons of bitches who started this there."*

Then, seeing there was more to be done, he got to work. He knew both Juanita's mule and the two the killers had been riding could get by on their own once he unsaddled, unbridled, and got them started with bellies full of water and oats. He didn't give a damn about the two dead company men, but he buried them as well, lest the buzzards disturb Juanita's final resting place or, worse yet, lead anyone else to the dirty sons of bitches.

CHAPTER
SEVEN

By the time he'd tidied up around the forlorn little
gypsy cart he'd cooled down a mite and the desert had
heated up a heap. The sky was still cloudy, but as the
noonday sun lashed down through gaps in the overcast it
served to remind him just how hot and dry it could get
in these parts and that there was only so much water a
mule could carry along with its rider and his gear. So
before he mounted up to ride he spread all of Lockwood's doodled charts flat on the ground in the skimpy
shade of the cart to consider his options.

He had his story. Or such a story as there was, at any
rate. Of course, the smartest move would be a beeline
back to El Cento and the first train out. He could report
the murder of Juanita to the law and let them worry
about it. But he knew they'd take as much action about
the death of a doubtless illegal immigrant as they had
about the shooting of Herbert Lockwood in front of witnesses. Nobody was allowed to duel in public in Frisco

or even Dodge these days, but the west was as wild as ever in some of its more primitive parts.

He knew he was thinking more primitive than smart as he made his decision and rolled up the charts again. He was a newspaperman, not a professional killer. But somebody had to bring the sons of bitches to justice, and he was likely the only man in these parts with a fast draw and a steady aim who wasn't on the payroll of the railroad and the water lords. So he forked himself aboard his mount and beelined for the work camp of the water oufit, loaded for bear and mad as hell.

He had his own pocket compass and there was nothing in his way but a heap of empty miles. How many miles depended on just how accurate Lockwood's spidery scribbles panned out. The engineer had left the forward diggings some days ago. By this time, even at pick and shovel speed, the more innocent laborers of the outfit should be farther west. But since how far west was up for grabs, Stringer made for a spot on the map where Lockwood had told him to Remember the Alamo. Stringer had only a fuzzy notion of what the ill-fated Lockwood must have had in mind. Since he'd been fired, about the time he'd shown his notations to somebody, that somebody might still be found in or about the work camp. Perhaps the rascal would tell him, when they met, why he'd fired Lockwood and, when that hadn't shut the poor cuss up, had him murdered.

There was no doubt in Stringer's mind now that the so-called shoot-out with a notorious gunslick had been murder, whether the victim had known he was being murdered or not. The average man, even an outdoors man with some experience at shooting cans off fence posts, had as much chance against a hired gun as a pussy cat against a bulldog. Nobody hired guns unless they were good. As Stringer had just had to prove, there was a lot more to gunfighting than just standing there pretending you were Wyatt Earp at the O. K. Corral. Having covered that story, Stringer knew it had been more complicated than old Wyatt now boasted at that classic shoot-out years ago.

Unless he was lucky as hell, the winner always had some edge in a fight. The thing that distinguished the true gunslick from his average victim was that from the beginning he could see who had the edge and knew exactly when and how to act on it. A lot of nonsense had been written by recent pulp and nickelodian "experts" about some so-called "Code of the West." And men who'd never heard a shot fired in anger were prone to enshrine homicidal lunatics like Clay Allison or nasty little back-shooters like Billy the Kid, even as they scoffed at braver men than they'd ever be who'd used common sense when the odds were against them.

It was probably true that James Butler Hickock had declined an invitation to a main street one-on-one with James Wesley Hardin that time. Who but a suicidal maniac would want to step outside into who-knew-what when he was forted up so good in a saloon with his back to the wall and two guns between him and the door. The wise-asses neglected to add that Hardin never chose to come in through that barroom door, for all his claims about wanting to have it out with Wild Bill. They just didn't know how the real thing was. A shoot-out was not a game between kids with cap pistols. Nobody who'd ever lived through such a gut-churning spell of sheer terror felt any need to offer anyone a sporting chance the next time he found his fool self betting his own life on the outcome.

Poor old Pat Garrett had good reason to turn morose and bitter in his declining years. Penny dreadful writers who'd never been west of the Big Muddy had used Garrett's own truthful account of his Lincoln County adventures to pillory the poor old lawman for nailing the notorious young killer a lot more fair and square than the Kid had done when he shot the previous sheriff from ambush. Garett and the Kid had met face to face, in Pete Maxwell's dark bedroom, and the only edge either had was that the Kid had spoken first and had given his location away when he asked Garrett who the hell he was. Garrett had openly admitted doing what anyone else with a lick of common sense would have done. He'd fired his six-gun instead of his mouth. The Kid had still managed to draw his own gun on the way down with a bullet in his heart. It was stupid to consider the notion that the Kid would have given old Pat "a fair chance" had their positions been reversed, and Lockwood had been stupid if he'd really expected a fair chance from Cactus Jack. Stringer hadn't been there, of course. But he could picture a dozen ways it might have happened. He knew a lot of gunslicks who enjoyed a rep for shoot-outs didn't exactly announce their intentions ahead of time. It was just as easy, and a lot safer, to simply engage a man in conversation out in the street, out of earshot of any witness, and then simply draw and drill him without warning. With the dead man in no position to dispute the killer's own version, it was easy enough to make the argument leading to the resultant "fair fight." Stringer made a mental note to hold any friendly discussion about the weather when and if he met up with Cactus Jack. For while he was madder about they way they'd treated poor little Juanita back there, he knew the death of Lockwood was tied in with hers. The same mastermind had to have given the orders. Neither Cactus Jack nor those two he'd just had to plant would have wandered about killing total strangers just for the hell of it.

The day on the desert wore on. He didn't seem to be getting anywhere as he walked, trotted, and rested his mule hour after hour. The jagged crests of the Sierra Chocolate to the east seemed to recede as fast as he approached them. Juanita's gypsy cart had slowly shrunk to a tiny dot and then winked out of sight behind him. But the flat expanse of greasewood all around looked just the same. If the Colorado Desert didn't kill a man, it sure tended to bore him to death. The Mojave had Joshua trees to ride past and the Sonora had all sorts of interesting cactus. The Colorado was just tedious and hence perhaps more dangerous. Ominous tales were still told of wagon parties who'd taken "short cuts" off the known and occasionally traveled trails. Every now and again some prospector came across an old sun-bleached wagonload of mummified '49ers, or even an earlier prospector, dried-up burro and all. The almost uniformly level greasewood shimmered like a sea, from slate-blue to black, making anything less than a mile away hard to make out. And there were an awful lot of miles out here.

Hence, when Stringer first spotted an unusual dot ahead of him he had to ride almost another hour before he made it out as a sunflower windmill, its new galvinized blades turning lazily in the tricky light of the overcast sunset. He resisted the impulse to spur his mule to a quicker pace. On the desert, it was always better to get there than to get there sudden. As the windmill grew with maddening slowness, he could make out the new tin roofing of the house and barn beside it. His mule smelled water and began to press forward. Stringer wasn't about to ride out of the desert at full gallop and likely scare some poor nester spitless. So he reined in, fired a shot up at the overcast sky, and rode in at a more polite trot.

As he reached the cleared door yard of the spread he found a man, a woman, three kids, and a couple of Mex or Indian hands lined up out front for his inspection and, judging from the casual rifle cradled in the nester's elbow-crook, vice versa.

He reined in. "Howdy. I'd be, ah, Don MacEwen. I'm trying to get to that big water outfit's work camp in case they may still be hiring."

The nester informed him, "I doubt you'll make it this side of sundown and change on that jaded mule. We're talking close to fifteen miles cut up with fencing and irrigation ditches. You and your mount are welcome to bed down in the barn for the night."

His once-pretty but now sun-bleached wife chimed in. "We're the Coopers—Fred and Doris. Our kids, here, answer to Sarah, Betty, and Fred Junior. These other gents would be the Gomez brothers. You're just in time for supper. Iffen you like, you can wash up by our kitchen door after you see to your mule, Mister Mac-Ewen."

He thanked her politely and, dismounting, led the mule toward the barn. One of the Mex hands fell in beside him to help. As they unsaddled, watered, and fed the mule in the barn, Stringer had the chance to ask the helpful Mex how much he ought to offer for the unexpected hospitality.

The Mex replied sharply, "No, señor, no money. La Señora is most sensitive about dinero. I fear they have put their life savings into this new spread and, as you shall see, the food they have to share will be simple fare. If you wish to show your gratitude, just do not ask for second helpings."

Stringer said he understood, and as they walked back to the house to run some water over their hands he pumped the hired hand for information about his hosts.

It seemed that the young family had sunk everything they owned into the purchase and improvement of this full section at the north end of a sort of skinny irrigation ditch, and whether they made it or not depended on the forty acres of cash crop they'd just drilled in. When Stringer asked about the windmill Gomez explained it didn't pump ground water since there was no ground water. The grade here was so flat, the loquacious Mexican told Stringer, that water had to be pumped from the feeder ditch to the fields and up to an attic tank that fed the tap they were using. Now Stringer understood why the washwater had felt so warm.

Dinner, as he had been warned, was meager and plain, boiled spuds, beans, a mighty skinny slice of raisin pie, and even thinner coffee. After dinner, while Mrs. Cooper and the two daughters did the dishes, Fred Cooper and his young son took Stringer for a stroll around the family estate. Most of it was still covered with greasewood which Big Fred said was a bitch to grub up. "However," he added, "our neighbors to the south have a steam tractor. Come some cash I mean to hire it to plow these infernal roots right. You have to kill every root and then soak the soil deep, more'n once, afore anything else will grow in it."

Stringer knew better than to ask why Cooper didn't want to ask a new neighbor for the free loan of his tractor. Instead, he inquired about the amount of water it took to farm such soil and, more casually, how much the Southern Pacific was charging an acre-foot for the same.

Cooper explained, "We didn't buy this section off the railroad. Got it at better terms off Imperial Land Management in Yuma. The water comes with, for the first year or more. They say once they have the whole irrigation scheme laid in and metered, our water ought to cost us less than a dollar an acre-foot. I reckon we can live with that." Stringer knew the man already had a lot of worries, so he felt he had no call to ask what Cooper and the other suckers would do if the water lords who had them at their mercy decided to charge more.

By now they'd come to a ditch about four feet wide and filled almost to the top with still, scummy water. Cooper frowned. "Haven't had much wind, lately, so that water's far too high." Then he turned to his son and said, "You'd best run down to the gate and spill some, Freddy."

His young son, already bored with the men's conversation, was only too happy to oblige. He ran on ahead as Stringer and his father followed along the already weed-grown edge of the ditch. When they caught up with the boy, Stringer watched him crank the wheel of a wood and angle-iron floodgate, damming the water behind it. As brown ditch water ran out in a widespread fan, Stringer noticed it didn't seem bound for anywhere in particular. Seeing his visitor's interest, Cooper explained, "You can see how flat the grade is. They only ditched this far north. They told us that once our drainage runs down such grade as there is a spell, it'll dig its own channel. Meanwhile, it just sort of oozes off toward Salton's Sink. It soaks in long before it can get there, of course."

Stringer turned to stare at the southern horizon as he absently rolled a smoke. "No offense," he observed, "but if this ditch runs as much as ten miles from the main feeder, it must start out a heap wider." Cooper said it surely did, since it had to feed eight or ten other fair-sized spreads before it trickled on to this one.

"What happens if there's a real rain, or someone sends too much water down this way for your ditches to handle," Stringer asked him. "I don't see no place for all that excess water to drain to."

Cooper shrugged. "Hell, it'll just soak in. This here desert silt is like blotting paper. There's no limit to how much water it can absorb. I have to water my beans and barley just about every day."

Stringer sealed his smoke and lit it. After he had drawn a few puffs, he observed as casually as possible, "It's a good thing you're getting so much water free then. As to blotting paper, there's a limit to how much ink a blotter will soak up before it commences to puddle all over your desk."

It was the sharp-eared kid, cuss his curious hide, who picked up on Stringer's words, asking him how come he knew so much about writing desks. Had Stringer wanted them to know he was a writer he'd have already told them so. So he cussed himself silently for the slip and explained he'd been to high school in his misspent youth.

By now the muddy puddle on the south side of the flood gate had formed a vast but only inches-deep spread of water. Despite this, the water in the deeper ditch had only dropped a couple of inches, and Cooper observed glumly that it soaked in faster when there hadn't been any rain. But since there wasn't much more anyone could do about it, the men went back to the house.

The next morning, after a good night's sleep in the Cooper's hay loft and a mighty poor breakfast at their table, Stringer rode on.

He'd ridden no more than a mile along the irrigation ditch before he came upon another gent standing ankle-deep in what looked to be a half acre of mud. The nester was cussing at the floodgate wheel he'd cranked all the way up to no avail. Beyond him, on slightly higher ground, stood a big stream tractor with its brass polished and its wheels freshly painted a bright fire-engine red. Stringer reined in at pistol range to call out, "Morning. I'd be Don MacEwen, and with your permission I'd like to cross your land. I'm bound for the work camp to the south."

The nester nodded graciously. "Ride anywhere you like as long as it ain't over my wife and kids, stranger. I'm W. R. Brown and I'm at peace with everyone in the world this morning but my disconsiderate neighbors to the north. That damned Cooper has his damned floodgate closed after all that rain, and opening this one hasn't done me a lick of good, as you can see."

"I just come from the Cooper place," Stringer told the man. "I can tell you for a fact that your neighbor opened his floodgate last night. He ain't the problem here. The problem both of you have is that once you get to the north end of this ditch, the water has no place to drain when and if the ground is too wet to just soak it up." He hesitated a moment, then decided to speak up anyway. "Do you mind if I make a suggestion?"

Brown told him to suggest away, since anything beat standing in a mud puddle.

"I'm no engineer," Stringer said. "But as I see it, the water company counted on the natural slope to the north to drain away excess water. It may, sooner or later. Meanwhile it's not much of a slope. So if I were you and Cooper I'd use that handsome tractor yonder to plow a deep furrow through and beyond that slight dip north of Cooper's floodgate. Nobody seems to be living there but lizards. A quarter mile of furrow ought to soak up a lot more water than the sun-baked surface and, who knows, you might even find another dip out there to use as a soak-in."

W. R. Brown was a man who could think on his feet,

which may have explained why he looked more prosperous than his ragged-ass neighbor to the north. He said, "By gum, that sure might help. But, seeing you seem to be on good terms with Cooper, would you mind approaching him about it for me? Me and my woman don't seem to meet their fancy for some reason. We sent one of the kids over with a cherry pie when they moved in. But they never even thanked us."

Stringer smiled understandingly. "New neighbors can take some getting used to. Still, I think it would be better if you and Cooper worked it out man to man. Since you seem willing to take my advice about drainage, are we talking man to man, no woman allowed, about what could have caused some misunderstanding betwixt you and the Coopers?"

Brown said he was listening and that his old woman didn't have to know everything. So Stringer explained. "They're decent folk. But they're poor as well. As one man to another, you surely know how shitty it makes a man feel when he can't spring for a round of drinks when it's his turn. Cooper admires you and your fine tractor. He told me so. I suspect he's just a mite jealous of you, in fact. He says that when and if he ever has the money he means to approach you for the hiring of your machine. Meanwhile, since he's broke, he feels no call to. His wife was no doubt shy about thanking your wife for that cherry pie because she had no way to thank her proper. I doubt they got a cup of sugar to spare. Do you follow my drift?"

Brown nodded in understanding. "I sure do. I had them down as natural stuck-ups and I thank you for setting me straight, old son. How come Cooper said he wanted to borrow my tractor?"

Stringer replied, "He never said he wanted to borrow

it. He said he'd like to hire it to grub out greasewood. Like I said, they're poor but proud."

Brown snorted at the notion. "Hell, all it takes to run old Betsy, as I calls her, is water and the free firewood all about. What if I was to start by just asking him permit to cross his land with my old Betsy to run some drainage out across the desert? We'd naturally get to talking and I could offer the use of the tractor later. How does that sound to a gent who seems to know Cooper better than me?"

Stringer said, "Right neighborly, Mister Brown. Well, it's been nice talking with you. But I got to get it on up the road now."

So they parted friendly and Stringer rode on, feeling even madder at the water company. Both the nesters he'd talked to so far had struck him as decent, hard-working folk, suckered out here to sink or swim, dumb as that sounded, in the middle of a damned near worthless desert. He saw now what Lockwood had been so concerned about. The engineer had no doubt overstated the dangers of draining ditch water the wrong way, since there seemed no way the water could do anything but spread out, a few inches deep, on all this nearly dead-flat land. But it only took a few inches of floodwater to drown a standing crop and drive snakes and worse from miles around into any house surrounded by any depth of unexpected water. The poor farmers investing in the scheme were more likely to be wiped out financially than drowned. But going broke could hurt almost as bad when one had a wife and kids to worry about.

By the time he reached the next section, the water in the ditch stood just about right. He only stopped there long enough to water his mule and chat a spell. He had to do the same at the next spread, and the one after that, since a stranger riding past without so much as a howdy struck most country folk as stuck-up if not suspicious.

He could tell he was gradually getting higher because, while he couldn't see any change in the grade, nobody this close to the rail and main water lines seemed to have noticed any standing water on their spreads after yesterday's unexpected rain.

Everyone he passed treated him decent. He was even forced to stop for coffee and cake later in the afternoon. And with each visit he heard tales of being dusted out in Kansas or of coming all the way out from the Ohio Valley because the price of land back east was so high these days. Most of the newcomers were young farmers, just starting out, with kids too bitty to really help. Some had taken on Mex hired hands. Stringer liked them too. Like most Anglo natives of the Southwest, he'd been reared to feel, rightly or wrongly, that while some Mexicans seemed ornery by nature, no Mex who was willing to work could be all bad, and the harder workers tended to be natural gentlemen with shy, sincere good manners. He hated to think that all the hard work both ethnic groups were putting into this project might turn out to be a flim-flam. Nobody he talked to had ever read *The Octopus* by Frank Norris. Hence it hadn't occurred to them they were captives of an oddly run water monopoly. He found it interesting, however, that so far he hadn't met a native Californian who'd bought a speck of land out here. He wondered if he would find out what the Octopus might have in mind for *these* poor greenhorns.

One of Lockwood's survey maps put both the railroad line and main feeder canal almost anywhere ahead of him now. The tracks of the S. P. had been laid across the desert years ago. The fool canal running out across the desert from the Colorado, just about where it met the Gila, got fatter and ran more twisty than the

tracks. Running water was a lot better at reading any
slope at all than the human eye. The irrigation lines
branching off the main feeder canal ran both north and
south, through railroad culverts when necessary. It
seemed obvious the water outfits and the Southern Pacific had to be in cahoots if the Huntington clan had
given permission to run water under its tracks.

Juanita had intimated that Lockwood had a drinking
problem. That, along with a habit of telling his bosses
they were digging their ditches all wrong, would have
explained their firing him easy enough. Stringer would
have accepted Lockwood's news tip as no more than the
word of a drunken worrywart, if they'd had the sense to
let things go at that. But they hadn't. They'd tried to kill
him, and they'd been successful in killing Lockwood
and Juanita. So there had to be more to the tale. Something that didn't show on paper.

Toward late afternoon, Stringer finally spied the forward work camp in the distance. A dotted line on the
southern skyline, farther west than he'd originally esti-
mated, materialized into a massive steam shovel and a
mess of tent tops as he crossed the railroad and rode
toward it. As he rode into the tent city, he spied a saloon
sign and decided that was as good a place to start as any.

The camp, while portable, was set up pretty good.
There was a watering trough for his mule by the hitching rail in front of the saloon tent, and when he ducked
inside he saw they had a real bar set up, with chairs and
tables and even a piano spread across the bare dirt floor.
There weren't many other customers, this still being a
working hour. Nobody was playing the piano and a
once-pretty fancy-gal at one end of the bar flashed a
heap of gold teeth and fake eyelashes at Stringer until
she saw he only seemed to want a beer.

The wiry barkeep who served him waited pointedly

for Stringer to lay some coinage on the bar before he smiled. "It pays to be cautious," he explained. "You just get off work, son?"

Stringer sipped some suds before he answered. "Just got here in hopes of finding some. Would you know who I'd want to talk to about that?"

The barkeep told him to look for a gent called Blacky over by the steam shovel. Stringer finished the beer, deciding they didn't give much for a whole nickel, and ducked back out into the harsh sunlight. He left his mule where it was and ambled toward the huffing steam shovel. His path took him close enough to the water course it had already dug to notice with interest how deep the dark water stood in the big ditch. Had he been in charge he'd have been dumping the spoil north instead of south of the canal, just in case. But he wasn't in charge, so he just joined the cluster of gents standing near the steam shovel as it picked up yet another great mouthful of soft desert silt and dropped it on the far side. He asked if anyone there might be Blacky. One of the onlookers pointed to a nearby tent and told him he might find the project supervisor there.

He did. The dark Irish gent seated at a chart table just inside admitted to being Blacky Burke. The heavier-set gent scowling at Stringer from a nearby camp chair was the one he'd backed down in El Centro in front of Juanita. Stringer nodded pleasantly and drawled, "Howdy. I figured I might find you here."

"That's him, the pistolero I had so much trouble with in El Centro," the burly man nearly shouted.

Blacky Burke stared soberly up at Stringer. "Who are you and how come my security man, Gus, here, had so much trouble with you?"

Stringer smiled and said, "Call me Don MacEwen. I didn't know this cuss was working for you. I thought he just liked to beat up women. It's been my experience you can get more out of ladies by sweet-talking 'em. Are you boys still interested in them papers she had stowed in her gypsy cart?"

Gus growled deep in his throat. But Burke ignored him and eyed his visitor with speculation. "We might be, MacEwen. Are you saying you have such papers on you?"

Stringer patted the front of his denim jacket. "I sure do. Like I said, sweet-talking will get a man further with a gal in the end than yelling at her."

Burke grimaced, but replied friendly enough, "What can I tell you? Good help can be hard to find. How much do you want for 'em, MacEwen?"

"Nothing," Stringer drawled. "They seem to be your property."

Stringer was not surprised to see Black Burke smiling up at him almost sweetly as he hauled out the dead engineer's papers and handed them across the chart table. Then, as Burke hurriedly spread them out, Stringer added, "I could use a job, if you're still hiring. The deal I hoped to make in town never panned out."

Burke didn't answer until he'd scanned the charts Lockwood had scribbled on and erased a couple of lines. "We may be hiring," he said cautiously. "What can you do? No offense, but you don't look like a born ditchdigger to me."

"I'm not. I used to ride top hand. Then I found out some outfits will pay more for a man who's good with a gun as well," Stringer informed him.

The hired gun called Gus broke in, addressing his boss. "You don't want this one, Blacky. He's a fresh-mouthed saddle tramp and no more."

Stringer smiled pleasantly at him, asking none too

politely, "Is that how come I backed you down so easy, you tin-horn nothing-much?"

As Gus half rose from his chair, Burke growled. "Not in here if you boys want to have it out."

"How about it, Gus," Stringer taunted. "You want to have it out again? You sort of let me down the last time."

Gus sat back down, muttering about damned fools. Burke smiled as if pleased. "As a matter of fact, Mac-Ewen, we're missing a couple of security men. I don't suppose you met up with an Anglo called Wordsworth and a Pima called Chino in your travels?"

Stringer made a sincere effort to look as if he was really thinking hard about that before he shrugged and replied, "I just can't say I have. You sent 'em to El Centro?"

"After you, as a matter of fact." Burke smiled again. "They should have been back by now."

Stringer insisted, in all honesty, that he'd met no such gents in town.

Gus growled, "They were after you, that gal, and them same papers Lockwood rode off with. How do we know they didn't catch up with you, and lose?"

Stringer snorted in disgust. "Oh, sure. After I shot it out with two men, to prevent you ever seeing those papers again, I just naturally felt it my duty to bring the papers to the boss man here. You must read a lot of mystery stories, Gus. Why don't you explain my mysterious motives to me? You must be stupid if you think anyone would shoot it out with two company dicks and then ride in to ask the same company for a job."

Burke chuckled at the picture, but asked Stringer shrewdly, "What did possess you to bring me those papers after you refused to let Gus, here, have them?"

Stringer tried to keep his voice light as he shrugged

and answered Burke. "I didn't know what he wanted. After I'd crawfished your pet ape away and, like I said, sweet-talked the little lady instead of trying to scare her, Lockwood's Mexican gal-friend showed me them. She didn't know why they were important to you, anymore than I did. I just helped myself when we parted friendly."

Burke said, "I see. What did you make out of them? Surely you must have looked them over before you decided to be so generous."

Stringer nodded. "I saw right off they were charts with spiderwebs penciled on 'em. If they'd looked like treasure maps, I'd have hung on to 'em. If they'd looked like evidence of anything sneaky, they'd have cost you more just now. I don't mind saying I'm still curious about what all the fuss is about. How come a mess of survey maps you could likely pick up cheap enough were all that valuable to you?"

Burke's face was innocence itself as he answered Stringer, "They were company property. Lockwood had no right to keep them when I had to fire him for drinking on the job. Some of these so-called spider lines show work we've done or mean to do. Without them we'd have had to run more survey work, and that's expensive." He rolled up the maps, indicating that was the end of any more explanation. "Now, we pay our security men five dollars a day. Gus, here, will see to your company badge and register you with Arizona Territory as a licensed private detective. You'll be working under him."

Gus started to object again, but Burke shot him a warning look. "If you don't like it, shoot it out with him. I just said good help is hard to find. If you're afraid to fight him, he may be just the sort of help I'm looking for."

When Gus didn't answer, the camp boss turned back to Stringer and asked more mildly, "How about it, Mac-Ewen? Are you willing to take orders from Gus if he's willing to let by-gones be by-gones?"

Stringer said, "Sure. I never fight anyone who doesn't want to fight with me, ah, boss. Is it too much to ask who else I might have to fight around here? Five dollars a day sounds like you're expecting serious fighting."

Burke said flatly, "We pay top wages for top guns. You'll find out who you may or may not be fighting when the time comes."

So that was how the outfit that had tried to have Stringer killed, more than once, wound up putting him on its payroll.

CHAPTER
EIGHT

Gus sullenly led Stringer to the nearby paymaster's tent and left him in the care of fussy little coot who asked so many fool questions that Stringer feared they suspected him until he decided the priss was likely just in love with his own overly neat penmanship. Stringer was hard put to come up with details he'd be able to recall as to his last dozen mailing addresses and previous employers. He'd chosen Donald MacEwen as a handy alias because he'd talked to some friendly member of the Frisco P. D. about the common mistakes folk made when picking a new name. The disadvantages of "Smith" and "Jones" were obvious. The all-time smartest alias was a hard-to-spell ethnic name from a different background than one's own, since few expected an Irishman to come up with a German name, a German to use an Armenian name, and so forth. But Stringer had taken the less complicated route of adopting the first name of a favorite uncle, and MacEwen of course meant "Son of Ewen" which he was. The same helpful detective had explained that the more foolproof total switch could lead to foolish slips before a new name settled in. Stringer knew that should someone call out his uncle's or his father's name unexpected he'd be likely to turn and respond in a normal fashion instead of just walking on as if he didn't know his own fool name. Besides, most folks thought any name with a Mac was Irish, and there were more Irish cowhands and railroad workers than one had time to brood about.

The paymaster rummaged about in a drawer in vain for a spare badge and said he'd have to get one for Stringer from Yuma, along with some proper I.D. "Anyway," he added with a sniff, "nobody will challenge your authority in camp. Most of our workers are illiterate Mexicans. Just don't get into fights off the reservation until we can get you fixed up with proper I.D. I need your John Hancock on this card for the paybook. Next payday will be a week and a half away."

Stringer signed Donald MacEwen in as natural a manner as he could manage and that seemed to be that. Just then a lean and hungry-looking individual dressed in jeans, black shirt, charcoal Stetson and two Colt .45s in a buscadero tie-down rig ducked into the tent. He greeted Stringer curtly. "Gus told me to show you about and help you get settled in. I'd be Sean Donovan, better known as Cactus Jack."

Stringer shook the hand the killer held out to him. He'd expected Cactus Jack to look more like the burly bully Gus. The almost civilized Cactus Jack shook firmly but without the unspoken challenge of the usual bully. His expression was neither warm nor nasty. Stringer sensed the notorious gunslick was simply a cold fish, so sure of himself that he didn't care whether anyone liked him or feared him. He just did what they'd told him to do. He'd have no doubt come in now with both guns blazing and with no more emotion if that had been what the boss ordered.

As they stepped outside together, Stringer said the mule he'd ridden in had to come before anything else. So they strode over to the saloon tent. Stringer was braced for the usual cowhand comments on mules, but Cactus Jack said nothing as he waited for Stringer to untether his mount. Then he led them both to the roped-in remuda and ordered their young Mexican wrangler to see to the critter and put Stringer's saddle and gear in the tack tent on the far side. When Stringer made as if to help, Cactus Jack stopped him impatiently. "Don't. The greaser's paid to wrangle. You and me are paid to keep order in camp. Come on, I'll show you around. There's not much about this job you'll find complexicated. Us and our guns just have to be handy when the damnfool ditchdiggers act up. Most of 'em are Border Mex. They don't get out of line often, but when they do we got to move in fast and bust as few heads as it takes to stop the fight. The boss can't get much work outten a Mex we bust up really hard, see?"

Stringer agreed it made sense to nip fights in the bud and, as they strolled along the service road between the railroad tracks and canal, he began to revise his first impression of total chaos.

The canal ran more or less in line with the tracks, two hundred feet, or "an easy tote" as Donovan put it, south of the rail line. The tent city naturally lay between, the tents staked a mite haphazzardly for at least a quarter mile east and west. Most of the tents seemed to be army surplus, left over from the recent war with Spain. Cactus Jack explained that as work progressed toward the west the tents were repitched, sort of leap frog, since the one farthest east was always the one farthest from the work face. It was up to whoever used a

tent as business or living quarters to decided when it
was time to pull up the stakes. Some workers were willing to walk farther to work in the morning than others.
Few of the tents were ever completely empty. Whenever
they could, Mexican laborers preferred to have their de-
pendents with them.

As some bare-assed little kids ran past them, Cactus
Jack explained indulgently that it made sense to let the
greasers drag their *mujeres* along. "I had to police an
all-stag and mostly Irish railroad construction camp one
time," he explained. "When men can't screw, they drink
and fight instead. This way's better, even if it does
complexicate the supply problem. After a hard day's
work in the sun our greasers just naturally roll over and
go to sleep after tearing off a piece. The only thing
wrong with having their mujeres along is that sometimes
they fight over the same one, and when men fight over
women they fight a lot meaner than your average drunk
Irishman. You got to drop the one with the knife fast lest
he cripple or kill half a dozen good shovel hands afore
they can get outten his way."

Stringer asked what the standing orders were if a
couple of workers were going at it with knives. Cactus
Jack said coolly, "You drop 'em both, of course. The
trouble with an overexcited Mex with a knife is that he
seldom knows when to stop. We had to gun one of their
women a week or so ago. She was a sassy little thing
with round heels and a welcome mat betwixt her thighs.
She caused a dozen serious fights afore we figured out
that she was causing 'em. Greasers are too romantic
natured to just take advantage of such free and easy
gals. Each and every one of 'em seems to think a gal he
laid the first night has to be his one true love forever."

Stringer frowned thoughtfully as they walked on and
asked, more casually than he really felt, "How come

you had to kill her? Couldn't you have just run her out of camp?"

Cactus Jack shrugged. "It was Gus as gunned her. He'd told her he would if she come back. We did run her out, more'n once. But she wouldn't stay run. So there was nothing else Gus could do. You can't let greasers defy you, you know."

Stringer repressed a shudder, asking how the other Hispanics had taken such harsh treatment of the woman. Cactus Jack said, "Oh, all the mujeres and some of them men were glad to see the last of her. It's hard as hell to get any sleep with damned fools fighting over pussy next door."

They came to where an irrigation ditch cut across their path to duck under the railroad tracks and run on to the north. It wasn't the one Stringer had followed out of the desert. He'd had to swing wide of that one when he'd seen the steam shovel off to his right. He didn't think much of the way this one slipped under the Southern Pacific's right of way. The twin tracks ran east and west along an embankment no higher than the shoulders of a man afoot. They'd just dumped crushed rock ahead as they'd crossed the soft, flat silt. The new culvert that the water now ran through was a jerry-rigged underpass constructed of railroad ties and a few bigger timbers to bear the weight of the trains rolling over it. Stringer knew wood didn't rot worth mention in the desert, but only because it rarely got wet.

"They ought to have a floodgate here. If those bottom ties stay wet all the time . . ." he started to point out.

"That's Blacky's business." Cactus Jack impatiently cut in.

So Stringer just shrugged and said, "You're right. It's not on my plate if a train crunches down through rotten underpinnings. It's not that big a drop in any case."

Cactus Jack agreed. "Right. We ain't working for the railroad. Our outfit is just out to ditch this fool desert, with a bonus for every extra mile ahead of the timetable set by Yuma. There's nothing in them tents across the way but mujeres and a yaller dog that snaps. You ready for a beer now?"

Stringer agreed that sounded like a grand notion. As they turned to saunter back the other way, Cactus Jack pursed his lips thoughtfully. "Gus says you was in El Centro a spell back. You heard about my visit no doubt?"

Stringer nodded soberly and replied, "I did. The few I talked to about it seemed to hold the view it was a fair fight, Jack."

The killer shrugged. "Fair or not, that damned fool had no call to cause Blacky so much trouble, Mac-Ewen." Then he got even more casual as he said, "Speaking of Macs. Do you recall another Mac called MacKail in connection with El Centro?"

Stringer made an effort to look unconcerned as he replied, truthfully enough, "I can't say anyone called MacKail was the topic of conversation when I was passing through. Are we supposed to be after him?"

Cactus Jack grimaced. "Likely not, now that Lockwood can't meet up with the pest. MacKail's a newspaperman with a rep for poking his nose into other gent's business. Lockwood bragged in town that he'd sent for MacKail and that once the story was in the newspapers Blacky Burke and some others would be in a heap of trouble."

Stringer tried to sound less interested than he was as he responded, "Do tell? I wonder what the rascal had in mind. I had a look at those company charts he rode off with before I brought 'em back to Blacky. All I could make out was that they said our outfit was digging over here. I don't see how that could get anyone in trouble. Hell, everyone riding back and forth across this desert must have noticed that swamping steam shovel and all this ditch water by now. What sort of secret do you reckon Lockwood aimed to spill to that nosy Mac-Phail?"

"The name's MacKail, not MacPhail," Cactus Jack corrected. "As to deep, dark secrets about construction out in open sight of cross-country travelers, your guess is as good as mine. Anyways, I've always been better with a gun than with a shovel."

There was more shoveling going on along the excavation to their left as they approached the salon tent. As far as Stringer could make it out, the steam shovel farther west was simply gouging out big gobs of dirt. Behind it, workers with shovels, hoes, and rakes had the task of smoothing the banks to a uniform width and more gentle angle. The silt's angle of repose seemed about thirty degrees. Had he been in charge he'd have considered waterproofing the bare mudbanks with cement or at least road tar. It still looked like rain, and while rain was rare out here it tended to make up for it when it arrived. He didn't ask Cactus Jack if those banks wouldn't erode like hell in a good gully-washer. He doubted even Black Burke wanted to think about that if he was getting paid by the mile instead of the future.

But that couldn't be what Lockwood had wanted to tell him. Gut-and-git was a code of the west more often followed than any code the writers of penny dreadfuls had ever come up with. Stringer had tried to sell many a feature on the Rape of the West. Every time he had, Sam Barca had pointed out that their readers didn't give a hoot about natural resources they couldn't get at. The land-loving Amish and landscape painters of the Hudson Valley hadn't been the folk who'd won the west. Few folk had trekked thousands of miles and fought at least that many Indians to admire the scenery and preserve the balance of nature. As Sam Barca liked to remark about the anguished John Muir and other worried naturalists, "A gent could study a butterfly just as well back east. Our readers come out here to get rich."

So there was no fresh news or a scandal worth reporting if all the water lords were up to out here was messing up a desert. Such doings were called progress and almost everyone out west approved. Nobody cared if range was overgrazed or how many trout streams got choked with mine waste as long as the men who got rich at the game paid their bills on time. The home range Stringer had grown up on was a lot more eroded than when the Miwok had gathered acorns on now open slopes of cheat grass and black mustard. The oyster beds of Frisco Bay that Jack London recalled so fondly were now fetid mudflats that stank of Frisco sewage when the tide was out. And nobody cared. So what in thunder could Blacky Burke be up to here that anyone might care about?

CHAPTER
NINE

The outfit had no time clocks. When it got light enough to see, the mostly Mexican crew was supposed to get to work. When it got too dark to see, they were allowed to knock off for the day. Most staggered home to eat the tortillas and beans prepared by their mujeres. A mess tent was set up to feed the Americanos who ran things, along with a few single Mexicans, who of course had their own table and had the expense of gringo rations deducted from their day wages.

Stringer got to eat free, which he thought just as well after he had tasted the cow camp grub they served. As an overlord who wasn't supposed to consort with mere Mexicans unless they were pretty and he wanted to, Stringer had been issued his own tent, and the laborers who'd been ordered to set it up for him seemed surprised but not displeased when he pitched in to help them. He'd have wanted to, even if he hadn't been so good-natured, because he saw right off that the kid driving the stakes was more used to living in an adobe.

Stringer tried not to hurt the young Mexican's feelings when he reset the stakes to hold in case the overcast sky had any wind in mind. It was now too dark, and too hopeless a task in any case, to concern himself with how many of the other tents along the canal were staked securely. If they blew down they blew down. He didn't think his would, now.

A couple more *peones* brought an army cot and the saddle and possibles he'd been worried about to the tent. He said he'd set up the cot and dismissed them with handshakes all around which they seemed to find surprising as well. Once he had his oil lantern going, Stringer went through his old gladstone. He'd seen right off that someone had forced the lock. But as he laid out his belongings on the dirt floor, he felt sure that thieving Mex kids hadn't gone through his personal things. Although nothing was missing, he was certainly glad he hadn't held out on Lockwood's papers or, God forbid, hung on to Lockwood's barometer.

He'd known before leaving Juanita's cart that everything south of that fossil beach had to be above mean sea level, and the few pencil lines Lockwood had added to the survey charts had been easy enough to memorize, for all they really told him. His press pass and other identification were on him, no longer in a wallet anyone might want to look at but tucked into the lining of his right boot. One of the nice things about Justins was that the thin, smooth inner lining was separate from the outside leather and one only had to pick out a few stitches with a pocket knife to have a handy hiding place.

He unfolded and set up the army cot. Then he covered it with the tarp and quilts he'd helped himself to before leaving the deserted gypsy cart. As he sat on his lonely new bed and rolled a smoke he wasn't sure whether he was smiling or only remembering the clean odors of poor little Juanita. Outside, someone was strumming a guitar and two *mujeres* were singing a sad *corrido* about another gal named Guirnaldita who'd died to save her honor. He lit the smoke, blew smoke out both nostrils like a pissed-off bull, and muttered to himself, "This is going to be swell. No later than nine o'clock, nerves all on edge, and I'm supposed to go to sleep with a dirge going on right outside."

He knew they'd shut up if he went out and told them to. Thinking he was a company gun, they'd jump in the canal if he told them to. But it wasn't their fault he was feeling blue and, come to study on it, scared skinny on top of it. So far it seemed he'd been accepted at face value. He'd noticed in the past that few folk expected a fairly well-known newspaperman to look so cow. The straw boss, Gus, had even nodded to him at suppertime, and the others likely thought a ragged stranger who was willing to draw on their top gunslick had to be cast from much the same metal.

But how long did he have? He was pushing his luck every extra minute he spent in this den of . . . what?

It was his infernal curiosity—that was what kept him from playing this game smart. He knew he could slip out now, while the slipping was still good. He only had to ride southwest to El Centro and board the first train that stopped there. It was the safe way to play it, the smart way to play it, but then he'd never find out what Lockwood had known, or, damn it, thought he knew, that was worth shedding blood over.

As Stringer sat there smoking and thinking about trains, it almost seemed as if he could hear one coming, chugging softly in time with that fool guitar outside. Then the guitar stopped and one of the gals who'd been singing laughed and called out, *"Ay, es el tren trabajo!"* Now Stringer could hear for sure the locomotive coming from the east, moaning at the dark clouds above.

He got up and ducked outside to see that the camp had come back to life, with everyone half dressed and some who should have been ashamed of themselves piling out to have a look-see as the work train tooted its whistle and rolled in to a slow stop. He ran into Gus, who cursed and told him, "Keep an eye on the damned kids. The little monkeys get in the way every way they can manage. The sons of bitchcs in Yuma might have had the courtesy to warn us in advance, goddamn their eyes."

Stringer had noticed the telegraph poles that ran along every main line in the country. But he hadn't known the camp had telegraph or telephone connections with their base camp closer to Yuma. He didn't comment. He knew Gus didn't like him to begin with, and he'd already figured a few things out just by keeping his mouth shut and his eyes and ears open.

As Gus moved up the line to cuss the train crew, Stringer yelled at a little girl who for some reason wanted to crawl between the train wheels. She shot him a scared look and ran off, to try somewhere else most likely.

He saw cases of supplies being unloaded all along the mostly flatcar combination. He stayed put so as not to get in the way in the tricky light. A couple of cars down they seemed to be running planks down to roll off something important. In the shifting flashes of firelight and inky shadows he could only make it out as something white and on wheels. A wagon to haul dirt most likely. He didn't move closer. He'd have plenty of time to look at it later.

A dark, trim silhouette materialized between Stringer and whatever else was going on over yonder. He'd just had time to make it out as a young woman dressed

Anglo in a travel duster and pith helmet before she spotted him as a gringo as well and approached him to ask charmingly, "I'm looking for a Mister Burke, sir." This was immediatley followed by, "Stringer MacKail! What are you doing here, for heaven's sake!"

He grabbed her elbow and drew her off to one side as he murmured, "Easy on that name, Kathy. We may not be among friends in these parts."

Kathy Doyle of the *Examiner* sniffed. "I'll be the judge of who my friends are here, you brute. The last time we met you screwed me silly and then scooped me on the death of Kid Curry!"

Stringer sighed and shook his head. "Kathy, your memory of such events fails to jibe with mine by miles. As I recall, we agreed to share the story as friendly rivals, and it was your own grand notion to beat me to the telegraph office and, come to study on it, leave me to await your return in vain, with a hell of a hard on."

She snapped, "Don't talk dirty. You know you played me false on that one, and I had a hell of time explaining how I scooped you and the *Sun* with a story that simply failed to match the facts."

He retorted, "Let that be a lesson to you. We made a deal and you tried to doublecross me. Cuss me for the fool I may be, but I'm still willing to make you the same offer. We work together, get the story, and wire it in together?"

"Leaving out my fair white body, which I swear you'll never abuse that way again, just what sort of story are we talking about *this* time?" she asked him warily.

Stringer looked around to make sure nobody could overhear them before he replied. "A real scoop. This water outfit has had two people killed and lost two hired guns to wastage so far. I'm still working on how come.

That's why I'm working here undercover, as a hired gun called Don MacEwen. How do you like it so far?"

She eyed him carefully and shot back, "I've a good mind to expose you as the sweet-talking fibber you are, Stuart MacKail."

But just then they were joined by Blacky Burke and the sullen Gus. It was Gus who asked, "What's going on here? Do you know this lady, MacEwen?"

A million years went by. Then the lovely but treacherous rival reporter trilled, "We were just talking about that, sir. I'm Kathy Doyle from the *San Francisco Examiner*. I feel sure I covered the trial of a Donald MacEwen in Colorado, one time. But he insists I have him mixed up with another train robber."

Blacky Burke chuckled and said, "So would I, in his place, ma'am. But just for the record, does old Don here look sort of familiar to you?"

She dimpled to them all, responding archly, "Far be it from me to dredge up a past a young man may be trying to live down. Maybe Donald has an identical twin. In any case, the last time I saw him, or thought I had, he got off on lack of evidence. Something must have happened to the witnesses against him. None of them ever showed up in court."

Then she tweaked Stringer's cheek. "And how did you manage that, you naughty boy?"

Stringer didn't answer. He didn't know whether he wanted to laugh or punch that fresh mouth of hers. But it seemed to go down well with Burke. He smiled thinly at Gus and said, "I reckon you were right to crawfish after all." Then he asked Kathy what they could do for her.

Her voice was just as light as she explained. "I have permission of the irrigation syndicate you're working for to visit this advance camp. My paper wants me to file an update on the progress you boys have been making out here in the desert. As you probably know, more than one investor has complained that this ambitious project doesn't seem to be working all that well."

Burke scowled. "Well, ma'am, we'll be pleased as punch to prove our critics dead wrong. Come sunrise you'll be able to see for yourself that we're miles west of where our subcontract calls for us to be right now."

A bug-eyed Mexican joined them to ask La Señorita where she wanted them to put her grand machine now that they had it down off the train. She handed him four bits with a gracious smile and told him to just leave it wherever it was for now. Then she turned back to the others to explain. "I brought my own transportation with me, a Stanley steam car. They told me in Yuma that one can drive all about out here in a horseless carriage."

Even Stringer wanted to have a look at such a modern marvel, so they all moved back to where, sure enough, a big four-seater sat between two tents, its long brass-trimmed hood and body bone-white and its red-tire wheels park-bench green. Blacky Burke kicked one of the red tires experimentally, declaring, "Well, I'll be swanned. Can you really handle this baby locomotive all by yourself, little lady?"

Kathy replied coolly, "I can. And I have far too much baggage for a horse to carry along with me. The steamer runs on water and kerosene. You'll have some I can purchase, of course?"

Burke bowed gallantly and assured her, "You can have all the lamp oil you need, ma'am. Gratis, of course. As for water, we got us a whole river of water here." Then he added, "MacEwen, you'd best make sure she don't fall in it and drown in this light. Since you two already know each other, I'm putting you in charge of making her feel welcome, MacEwen. Dragoon her a tent and as many *peones* as it takes to set her up comfortsome."

Kathy said she had her own tent in the trunk of her steamer. Burke opined how that was nice and drifted off with Gus to see the other unloadings, or perhaps because he wanted to avoid talking to a newspaperwoman any more than he had to.

Kathy turned to Stringer and pouted, "I think I've been snubbed!"

"I think so, too," he replied. "They left you in my care because I've satisfied them I'm just a drifting gunslick with no idea what they're really up to."

"Oh? And just what are they really up to, ah, Donald?" she asked.

Stringer replied, "I'm still working on it. Together we might be able to come up with something. You won't see anything by daylight that looks at all suspicious. I've already looked, with the freedom of the camp. Let's hope we can both look as dumb and they may slip up. You say you have a tent somewhere in this damned contraption?"

She said, "In the trunk. I'll show you. But don't make fun of my spunky huffer-puffer before you've see it scoot. I had a race with the S. P. Coaster coming down from the bay a few days ago and beat it across the Salinas Valley. On a straight stretch of road I can crank it up to seventy miles an hour!"

Stringer sighed. "I sure wish you'd stop lying to me just for practice, Kathy. Look here, I reckon we'd best set up your tent with this steamer betwixt us as chaperone. That heavy-set one called Gus doesn't like me and so . . ."

"I'll have you know," she cut in, "That I don't need a chaperone as far as *you're* concerned, sir! Just because you took unfair advantage of me that time gives you no right to take my favors for granted. So you can just forget any notions about creeping into my tent like a love-sick A–rab in the wee small hours!"

Stringer hauled her tent out and snorted in disgust. "I wasn't aware I was taking advantage of you. I'm glad you've been kind enough to set me straight. All this time I've been thinking you pulled a Delilah to steal that scoop on the Wild Bunch from poor, helpless me." His tone and words made her laugh despite herself.

The work train was backing off now, so Stringer was able to dragoon a half dozen workers to help him set up the fancy tent to Kathy's satisfaction and install all the gear she'd brought with her. Then she flounced inside without thanking anybody and lit her fancy Coleman lantern. It was one of those jobs that got pumped up like a bicycle tire, and it gave off more light than an Edison bulb, turning her tent into a sort of big, square Japanese lantern. He wondered if she was aware of the shadow show she was putting on inside as she took off her helmet and unpinned her hair. Knowing Kathy Doyle, he felt sure she did, and he knew she knew he was watching.

He saw the Mexicans watching as interestedly as him, and he told them curtly to knock it off and go back to their tents. They left, muttering about him being a spoil-sport. He leaned against the fender of her Stanley steamer, rolling a smoke, to make sure the whole damned camp didn't gather to gawk until the fool woman put out that damned light. He found it hard not to gawk himself as she slipped out of her duster, hauled her dress off over her head, and sat on her cot bare-assed, or close to it, to comb her long auburn hair. From out here, of course, he couldn't make out the color of her hair or see whether her naked skin was as creamy and smooth as it was that time up Colorado way. But even as a shadow show she was having an effect on Stringer's glands that he'd sworn she'd never have again. He wondered what effect he'd had on her glands that time. It was easier for a gal to fake such matters than it was for a man, and she'd certainly had all her wits about her when she'd lit out on him to wire the story in ahead of him. Though he had to chuckle when he recalled he hadn't given her the *whole* story, yet. Male news folk had to control their passions just a mite as well when playing slap and tickle with a determined rival.

He wondered if that had taught her a lesson. She surely was a smart little thing with a highly developed nose for news. He was going to have to work with her again, though, if only to keep her from exposing him. It was obvious she'd come out here working on a tip of her own, so she probably knew some details he didn't. The two of them made a good team as far as getting the story went. The problem was how in thunder he'd convince her it was naughty to doublecross a pard once she had a scoop in her hot little hands. For Kathy Doyle was one of those sweet little things who'd poison her mother and screw a snake for her very own by-line on an exclusive.

He'd just lit his Bull Durham when her Coleman lantern went out. It was just as well because a few drags later he was joined by Cactus Jack. The lean and hungry-looking gunslick walked once around the Stanley, marveling at how big it was next to the last horseless carriage he'd seen in Tucson one time, and then he joined Stringer near the head lamps to hook a boot over the front bumper. "They told me you was helping that lady from Yuma set up camp. Are you on guard or what?"

Stringer shrugged. "Thought I'd stand by and make

sure none of the kids pestered her until she'd trimmed her lamp. Why?"

Cactus Jack nodded at the now-dark tent. "I'd say she'd already done so. I've noticed you talk pretty good Spic dealing with our greasers."

"It's not such a hard lingo," Stringer said. "And first off you start by not calling 'em greasers. Anyways, what's this all about? You asking me for Spanish lessons at this infernal hour?"

Cactus Jack responded sheepishly. "Sort of. You see, there's some Spanish farm folk who've just set up near the feeder ditch on the far side of the tracks. I don't mean the greaser kind. They're a high-toned Spanish family who just come over from Santa Fe. They're white as you and me. The man of the family talks good American. But they got this daughter, Maria, who don't. I thought you might like to ride over yonder with me tonight and see if you could help me talk to her a mite."

Stringer shot a wistful glance at Kathy's blacked-out tent and asked, "Might your Maria have a friend?"

Cactus Jack look downright indignant as he protested, "It ain't that sort of situation. We're talking about a decent young gal. She's so pretty it hurts to just look at her. But I'm sure she ain't never been kissed. Her folks are friendly. They don't seem to mind me dropping by. But every time I try to talk to Miss Maria she just blushes and ducks into the house."

Stringer didn't answer. He was afraid he'd laugh as he pondered the picture.

"I only want to talk to her," Cactus Jack insisted. "To have you talk to her for me, leastways. I want you to tell her my intentions are honorable, see?"

Stringer was beginning to. Unbelievable as it seemed, he could see that even ogres must fall in love now and again. He took a thoughtful drag on his cigarette, choosing his words carefully before he asked the hired killer cautiously, "Has it crossed your mind that a gent in your line of work might be, well, too exciting a husband for a shy little Spanish gal of good family?"

Cactus Jack sighed. "It has. I used to be a fair roper afore I discovered the wages of sin paid so much better. I got me some money in the bank of Yuma, and I don't reckon it would kill me to take up cows again as long as I could hire some greaser vaqueros to do most of the work."

Stringer whistled thoughtfully. "Your Maria must be something, no offense. Are you talking about grazing stock on irrigated desert here, Jack? That's a mighty expensive way to feed cows."

The love-struck killer shook his head. "Hell, I ain't that dumb. Once they got all this land sold off and commence to meter the water the suckers will be hard put to make a living on fruits and nuts. But I know where I can pick up a nice little homespread in the Oklahoma Panhandle, if Miss Maria might be at all interested."

Stringer nodded. "She might be. You ain't deformed and you've yet to murder anyone in front of her. But if you're really serious about the gal I'd best give you a Spanish lesson after all."

Cactus Jack snorted. "I ain't got time to learn a whole new lingo, damn it. I want to marry up with Miss Maria as soon as I can!"

Stringer nodded. "I'm not talking about teaching you to speak Spanish. There's just some things you have to know before you even try sparking a lady of your Maria's background."

Cactus Jack said he was listening, so Stringer told him. "To begin with they remember the Alamo, too, and they're used to our kind leaping at their women with less than honorable intent. The young lady doubtless speaks better English than you, if she grew up in New Mexico wearing shoes. If you're really serious about her, you have to start by paying less attention to her and get on the good side of her father. She's not supposed to even look at you, save mayhaps over the top of a fan, until her old man says he won't kill you both if she does. You have to tell him right out that you admire his daughter and ask his permit to court her. If he admires you as much as you admire his daughter, you're home free. They'll never leave you alone with her of course. But once you've brought her some flowers, books, or candy you'll have less to say about getting out of the understanding than you might think. So make sure you mean it before you talk to her father and, if you do, just let nature take its course, see?"

Cactus Jack said he did and that he was fixing to ride over right this minute to propose to Miss Maria's father.

"Hold your horses, old son," Stringer warned him. "It's too late at night to call on quality folk uninvited. You're not supposed to act like a horny Texan anxious for some Mexican ass."

Cactus Jack snapped, "Easy, now, MacEwen. You are talking about the future Mrs. Donovan!"

Stringer shot back. "And you start by acting that way your own fool self. You ride over by broad day and get her father into a friendly discussion about the weather or whatever. Then you ask if his daughter's been spoken for. If he says she hasn't, it means he's following your drift and the rest comes natural. If he doesn't want you around, he'll tell you she's engaged whether she is nor not, see?"

Cactus Jack growled, "Courting Spanish gals sure sounds like a bewildersome chore. But what you say makes sense, now that I study back on some Mexican brothers I've had to fight in my wicked youth. I thank you for your Spanish lesson, MacEwen. For your sake I hope you ain't steered me wrong."

Stringer let that pass. He sensed that, unlike Gus, this one would be a hard man to back down, so there was no sense trying before one had to.

Cactus Jack strode off into the darkness to no doubt practice talking about the weather, and Stringer headed for his own tent before he could get in any more trouble.

CHAPTER
TEN

He didn't bother to light his lamp, so he didn't know he had company until he sat down on the cot, almost right in the lap of Kathy Doyle. He didn't know who she was until he'd grabbed her and almost punched her, demanding, *"Quien es?"*

She gasped and replied in her all too familiar voice, "Take it easy, for God's sake. I bruise too easily to wrestle with men your size, Stringer!"

He'd already determined she had nothing on but a terry-cloth robe, open down the front. So he just said, "Easy with names. Any wall can have ears and these are canvas. I thought you said you weren't receiving creeping Bedouins this evening, honey."

"I told you not to creep into *my* tent," she giggled. Then she added sternly, "but I didn't slip into your tent to be naughty, so keep those big hands to yourself. I just heard you talking to someone out there. What was all that about?"

He replied, "A love-sick assassin. I can't see his

pending engagement making the society pages of either of the papers we work for. But if you're here for business, let's get on with it. If you're ready to compare notes, suppose I tell you what I know so far, and you can take it from there."

She agreed, and he quickly brought her up to date on the tip from the late Lockwood and the adventures that had followed, leaving out some of the exercises he and Juanita had worked out on that skimpy bottom bunk in her gypsy cart.

By the time he'd finished, he could tell Kathy was hooked. So he made her tell why the *Examiner* had sent her out.

Apparently their tip had come from Sacramento, where a state senator had been raising ned about the Imperial Daydream, as he called the plan to irrigate the Imperial Valley. A lot of land, mostly railroad grant land, had been sold long before any waterworks seemed to be anywhere near them, and so a lot of new settlers had been bitching, loudly, about the dusty greasewood flats they appeared to be stuck with. Kathy had been sent to the Yuma headquarters of what she described as a water trust. She confided she'd been "just a little naughty" in Yuma when, after getting the usual runaround, she'd taken to listening in on telephone conversations and reading other people's mail.

"As I put it together, separate contractors have been digging all over the place out here in the desert," she explained. "This construction crew here had gotten way behind schedule under a project foreman who kept taking the advice of his surveyor, your poor Mister Lockwood. So they called him back to dig somewhere else and put our Blacky Burke in charge. In Yuma they seem very happy with the results. He's been digging away like crazy. But since I found out some of the big shots back in Yuma seem to be worried about their project just the same, I thought I'd come out here and see for myself. But I haven't seen anything so far," she shrugged. "Okay, mister, now it's your turn."

Stringer grimaced. "You'd have to be an engineer, like the one Burke fired, to tell whether he was crazy or not. Burke strikes me as a hard-driving roughneck who plays even rougher than he has to. I'm not ready to say whether he knows what he's doing yet. Old Herb Lockwood could have been just a nitpicker in the path of progress."

Kathy cut in. "They told me in Yuma he was a railroad construction man of the old school. Someone said something about Burke digging a waterway closer to the railroad tracks than they'd told him to. Does that mean anything to you?"

Stringer replied cautiously. "It might just mean he didn't like to haul supplies any farther than he had to. And I can see how a man who was more used to laying ties and tracks than surveying water tables would consider that a needless worry. I can also see why an earlier contractor who did worry more about such matters might have gotten behind schedule. It must be a bitch to survey little more than a yard, either way, across flats covered mostly by windblown dust and greasewood roots. Burke is being paid by the mile. He's a gut-and-gitter of the old school. If he can finish this diversion before the spring flooding along the Colorado, he'll be long gone before any mistakes he might have made show up. He no doubt figures the higher railroad bank to the north will stop any mild flooding in the meanwhile."

Kathy thought a minute. "All right, let's say our uncouth Blacky's cut a few corners to get the job done. Why would he want anyone killed to keep that news under wraps? You just said he's being paid by the mile, so surely they know back in Yuma where he more or less has to be, right?"

Stringer nodded. "I don't think they much care where he is, back in Yuma. The engineer in charge of all this nonsense walked off the job a while back and they're just sort of muddling through as best they can. We're already just west of the weird warning Lockwood wrote across Burke's march of progress and so far nothing's happened."

She asked Stringer what he was talking about and so, although he suspected he already might have revealed to a rival more than anyone with a lick of sense should have, he told her how Lockwood had warned everyone to "remember the Alamo" out here. "I wish I knew what the hell he meant by that," he mused.

Kathy Doyle hesitated. She'd been scooped by Stringer more often than she'd ever managed to scoop him. But in the end she told him. "Well, since we've agreed to share credits on this one, I may as well say I think I know. Back in Yuma I got to look at a huge wall map, all covered with contour lines and explaining the so-called hydrography of this delta. That's what they called it on that big survey map, a delta, not a desert."

He replied skeptically, "I know all that, honey. Get to the point." So she continued coyly. "I thought you'd forgotten that time we lost our heads. Anyway, the Alamo is a river—a once-upon-a-time river, that is. As the muddy waters of the Gila-Colorado pushed across the head of the gulf at right angles it ran this way and that, in a mess of different twisty river beds called the Alamo, the Bee, and New Rivers. Each bed would silt in after a time, so then the water would have to run some other way in turn. Once there was dry delta land all the way across, the main stream finally found a way to the sea. So that's been what we call the lower Colorado ever since. The old Alamo River never ran that way. It ran into Salton's Sink, to the north, until the whole valley just dried up as you see it now."

Stringer half closed his eyes to picture his present surroundings the way they might have been back in the Ice Age, when an even mightier and muddier Colorado had been sloshing all over these parts with a mind of its own. He nodded thoughtfully. "I knew we'd come up with something if we put our heads together. That has to be what Lockwood meant."

She answered demurely, "The results were sort of interesting the last time, you double-crossing brute. So what did that poor dead engineer really mean?"

Stringer explained, "Just what he wrote. Burke's already dug across the old bed of that fossil river, running north into that fossil sea. Nobody noticed, or at least nobody cared but old Herb. The old channel can't be more than a few inches deep now. Lockwood was afraid that since water runs downhill, even if downhill is only a few inches, a flash flood off the slightly higher flats to the south would naturally run along the old bed of the long-dead Alamo to mess things up here. I see now why Burke has been tossing the spoil to the south. It ought to dam any unwanted water coming this way, assuming we're not talking about rain you don't usually get out here. The surrounding desert would easily soak up six or so inches of rain before any of it got to running."

Kathy answered, "I can see that without a hydraulics degree. But I'll be cussed if I can see why a muddy work camp called for Blacky Burke to kill anyone."

Stringer explained, "He never killed anyone directly. He just told his hired guns he didn't want anyone reporting careless workmanship before he could finish the job, take the money, and run."

She said she didn't see much news in that, adding, "I've tried more than once to write an exposé on San Francisco construction inspectors. My editor says nobody will care unless and until their own house slides town Telegraph Hill."

Stringer nodded morosely. "I know the feeling. But Blacky Burke never worked in a pressroom. Unless we're missing something, I'd say he simply doesn't want to pay off any inspectors, company, state, or federal. He's just suffering a guilty conscience, knowing he's been bulling on across the desert to get paid by the mile and to hell with where all the water ever winds up. He doesn't know no paper in the country is likely to run a line on him until such time as he causes a total disaster worth reading about over breakfast by folk miles away with hardly any notion where the Imperial Valley might be."

Kathy observed sarcastically, "Pooh. Unless we can make a disaster happen, I'd say we both came down here on a snipe hunt."

Stringer agreed. "But Blacky doesn't know our editors. We could both be in a lot more danger than any story we could milk out of this tedious mess might justify. How far can that steamer of yours go on one boiler-full? I noticed you had it brought this far out on the desert by rail."

"I had to," she replied. "They told me water was a sometimes thing out here and I have to stop every fifty miles to cool her off and fill her up again. Why do you ask? Are you looking for a ride?"

He hesitated, then nodded. "I reckon I am. We're both pressing out luck the longer we stay out here with these unprincipled rascals. I doubt like hell that anyone's going to confess right out to killing anyone, but that's the only news angle either of our papers would be

interested in. So how about it, Kathy? This time you've
no reason to try and beat me to the wire, and I think we
could make El Centro on one good boiler charge. The
cross-country trains stop there and we could load your
steam buggy aboard a flatcar there, see?"

She pondered his proposal a moment. Then she nodded in agreement. "I like you better when we're not
fighting over a scoop. I'd be nervous about driving
across the desert alone in any case. I guess that makes
us friends again after all, right?"

He agreed he had no hard feelings. Then she proved
him a liar by shoving him off the cot, forking a leg
across him as he lay on his back, and getting to work on
his fly, saying, "I'd rather be on top than on this hard
ground, and that silly cot is just too frail and skinny for
real fun."

He'd just had time to agree before she'd impaled
herself on his erection, crooning. "Oh, that does feel
good. I'd forgotten how nicely hung you were, my
dear."

He laughed like hell but had to allow he'd forgotten
how nice she was built where it counted as well. She
sniffed and said she'd just known he couldn't be true to
her. Then she bounced on him enough to drive them
both loco en la cabeza and inspire him to haul the covers
off the cot, the duds off both of them, and to finish
right, with her on the bottom.

She said the earth under her rollicking rump didn't
seem to be solid cement after all, and proved it by
damned near bucking him off before they climaxed together. Then she giggled at him shyly and asked, "For
heaven's sake, aren't you going to kiss me even once
tonight?"

He did. He'd forgotten how nicely she did that, come
to study on it. That inspired them both to start moving

in time together in a sweeter sugar-and-spice way. There was a lot to be said for making love in old familiar places, if one didn't overdo it or forget how sneaky this sweet-loving little gal could be.

Later, as they lay there atop the quilts with her head resting on his shoulder and her free hand searching for further signs of life in his sated shaft, Kathy murmured, "I think our best bet would be for me to act dumb in the morning, let them feed me some banana oil, and then decide on a drive out across the desert. Naturally, I'd need you to guard me against snakes or worse and. . . . Let's see, I could write my tent off as travel expenses and nobody would notice if we slipped all my valuables in the trunk again. We'd be long gone before anyone got around to wondering when we'd be back. How does that sound to you, darling?"

He chuckled in mock horror. "Scary. You never let the wheels in that pretty little head of yours stop ticking, do you?"

She replied archly, "A girl has to look out for herself in this man's world. Do you think I could get this back up with a teeny-weeny French lesson or do you want to go to sleep, dear?" He said both sounded just grand.

So they were enjoying crimes against nature, or at least the statute laws of more than one fool state, while farther up the line Gus ducked into Blacky Burke's headquarters tent to report.

"You know what that newspaper gal and that rascal who calls hisself MacEwen are doing right this minute, boss?"

Burke cupped the mouthpiece of the telephone on his chart table in one large palm. "I can imagine. She's not bad looking and he already had the inside track with her. Hold the gossip a mite. I'm on the horn to Yuma and it sounds serious."

Gus found a seat and sat there fidgeting while Burke went on talking, or in fact mostly listening, until he hung up with a frown and told Gus, "That rain that passed over us here just hit the mountains to the northeast, and a hell of a lot harder. Yuma says the damned Colorado is in flood and the Gila's rising. I don't know what the hell they expect me to do about it. It's up to them to work the floodgates betwixt here and there."

Gus was interested in only one topic of conversation and it certainly wasn't rainstorms. He leaped back to his feet, insisting, "The two of 'em was screwing. I could tell as I was hunkered near his tent outside."

Blacky snapped back, "Damn it, Gus, I'm more worried about rising water than rising peckers right now."

But Gus pressed on. "That ain't all. They was talking about you. Talking mean. That jasper I warned you not to hire never come right out and said he was the famous Stringer MacKail. But from the way they was jawing about newspaper stories together I just can't see him as a train robber she recalled so fondly!"

Gus's information had caught Burke's attention at last. He pursed his lips and muttered, "Hmmm, one Mac does sound like another Mac when you study on it. Whoever he may be, I sure don't want him blabbing about me to any damned newspaper gal!"

With a wicked grin Gus asked, "You want me to gather Cactus Jack and some of the others now, Boss?"

Burke grimaced. "Don't be so crude. There's no way even Cactus Jack could pick a gunfight with a she-male the Yuma office knows it sent here. Come morning we'll show her around as sweet as anything and see if we can't put her aboard the first eastbound freight we can flag. She can't write mean things about us if she don't know anything, right?"

Gus agreed, then hesitated. "What about MacEwen, or whoever he is?"

Burke shrugged and replied, "Oh, we'd best do him in and plant him in the desert, no matter who the hell he may be."

CHAPTER
ELEVEN

It was just getting light again when Kathy nudged Stringer awake, demanding in a disgusted voice, "Have you been making wee-wee in your sleep, for heaven's sake?"

He yawned, felt the damp quilting they lay naked atop, and replied, "I might ask you the same thing, little darling. But I suspect we're both innocent. It's too damned cold and, Jesus!" he added, sitting up, "there's too damned *much* of it!"

She had to agree, as they both sat there in the cold, gray dawn observing the wet mud all around them. Even as they watched it seemed to be getting wetter. Stringer swore and helped Kathy up to the cot where they'd fortunately piled his duds and her robe. As they proceeded to get dressed, he told her, "You'd better sneak out, slip into that duster at least, and load up your steamer. This is no place for a lady right now. The damned canal is overflowing. I don't know why either."

He stomped on his boots, put on his hat and gun rig,

and ducked out to see if he'd guessed right.

He had. A silvery sheet of inch-deep water now extended from the canal to the railroad bank as far as the eye could see, and everything that wasn't under water seemed to be running around in circles screaming in Spanish. Few of the Mex kids were dressed, and more than one full-grown Mexican, male and female, were out in the open calling on their saints, Christian or Indian, to save them from this Biblical deluge which was now almost two inches deep in spots.

But Stringer knew inches of water still added up to a lot when it was spread, and apparently still rising, across one hell of a heap of territory. He sloshed down to the far end of camp where he found Cactus Jack Donovan and a dozen Mexicans shoveling dirt in the ditch leading through the railroad culvert. As he watched questioningly, Blacky Burke suddenly splashed past him, yelling angrily, "Are you out of your mind, Jack? We've got all the water we need on this side of the tracks. Let it run on through, you damned fool cowboy!"

Cactus Jack protested, "We can't! There's folk downstream and I'm mighty fond of one of 'em! Afore we just stopped it, it was gushing through like a zillion fire hoses, overflowing the ditch on the far side entire!"

Burke snorted in disgust and roared at the Mexicans in fair Spanish. Some were already scooping muck the other way as Burke told Cactus Jack, "We have even more folk on *this* side of the tracks. We built that culvert to drain water to the north, and anyone can see it has no other place to go, you idiot!"

Stringer left them to work it out as he hopped up on the railroad embankment for a look-see on the other side. He whistled at the sight before him. Brown water, not much deeper than what he'd just climbed out of, was boiling ominously out the far side of the culvert as it dug a progressively deeper channel for itself along the original unstabilized irrigation ditch. Way off, across the brushwood tops, he could make out the roofing of a homespread, though he couldn't tell how far the sheet of water had spread among the stems of the slate-gray greasewood. He dropped back down to rejoin the men arguing by the inside entrance of the timber culvert. He was dismayed to find himself now ankle-deep in water as he called out, "You're both right. There's one heap of water on its way to Salton's Sink right now. As it digs in and speeds up it could add up to a hell of a mess. But trying to hold it all on this side could add up to even worse."

He turned and told Cactus Jack, "Jack, you'd best ride hard and fast for your gal's place. If they have riding stock, have 'em mount up and ride west at right angles to the sheet flooding. If they don't have stock, make 'em run like hell. The grade's so gentle there's no way of telling just where it may go. But if it don't go down on this side fast, it just has to get worse!"

Cactus Jack lit out for the remuda. Stringer then turned to Burke and advised, "You'd best get every man and boy who can shovel dirt to cut through that spoil bank on the far side. It ought to drop the pressure building against this railroad bank some."

Burke looked sick as he replied, "It won't work. The ground to the south slopes *up!*"

But Stringer insisted, "It can't slope up that much. Its flat all the way to the damned ocean to the naked eye. Even if this water only spreads a few inches deep to the south, we're still talking lots of water. Where on earth could all of it have come from, as clear as the sky looks this morning?"

Burke swore under his breath. "They just called me

about it from Yuma. The goddamned flood crest of the goddamned old Gila has risen higher than it's ever been recorded afore. Higher than this goddamned desert, in fact." Then he yelled, "Where do you think you're going?" as Stringer splashed back the way he'd just come.

Without breaking stride, Stringer shouted back, "Donovan's right about there being folk on the far side of that railroad bank. Somebody has to warn them. The floodwater boiling through the culverts back down the line may not do more than water the fields sort of heavy. But if a section of the Southern Pacific goes with the flood crest behind it, I doubt there'll be time to build many arks!"

Stringer ran back to his tent to find Kathy Doyle sitting fully dressed and amazingly sedate behind the wheel of her Stanley steamer, now hubcap deep in ominously swirling water. He hastily gathered his own belongings, tossed them in the back seat, and climbed in beside her, soaked to the knees, tersely announcing, "Let's go, honey."

Kathy shook her head. "Not just yet. It takes a few minutes for the steam pressure to build up. That's the only disadvantage to steamers, next to an electric or gas buggy. Where are we supposed to drive, once we can, by the way? There seems to be more water down the tracks, as far as I can see and . . . oh, look at what that steam shovel seems to be doing up ahead!"

There was no seems-to about it as the big black pile of machinery slowly tilted backward toward the ditch it had been digging. Its front tracks undermined by swirling water, it picked up more speed and then suddenly belly-flopped into the wide but now invisible canal with a mighty splash, sending a wave of muddy water surging over the railroad embankment.

Stringer shouted to Kathy, "Pressure or no pressure you'd better get cracking before this water rises to your kerosene burners."

She said she'd try it on three-quarters pressure and threw open the throttle. The rear wheels spun madly in the mud and shot up twin rooster tails of muddy foam before they were on their way.

As the passenger seat tried to snap his spine, Stringer gasped, "I hope you're at least aiming this cannon ball. If you are, see if you can get us up and over the railroad bank."

She could. It was scary as hell, to a man more used to cow ponies, to tear up and over with all four wheels in the air a spine-jolting part of the time. As the more blasé Miss Doyle drove calmly south, flattening grease-wood bushes with her bumper at a respectable speed of fifty miles an hour, she asked again where they were headed now, adding, "I don't see anything out ahead of us but more of the same, dear."

Stringer didn't either, but he had reached a decision. "All right," he said, "let's see if we can cut across the front of that spreading water. Make it ten miles north and then swing east."

She said she'd try. He knew distances were hard to judge on the open desert, so he was surprised when she suddenly swung her steamer to the right. "We're ten miles from those tracks if my odometer still works," she explained. Then she asked almost plaintively, "Why are we doing this, dear?"

He answered tersely, "We may be able to warn folk to get to . . . son of a bitch, there's not any high ground to get to for miles! But at least we can make sure everyone's up and dressed and ready to climb ladders in a hurry."

Then, as they went on crashing through greasewood

and getting sprayed with muddy water, Kathy gasped, "Whee! I just turned into a speedboat! But no fooling, Stringer, ten miles out here, already?"

He replied, "It's moving shallow, but it's moving fast. Even faster than I figured, judging the grade by eye alone. Slow down. The water's moving fast enough to dig channels and carry a more serious amount of water. This'd be one hell of a time to find out if this thing floats."

"It doesn't," she said, as she slowed them to a crawl. Thanks to the almost silent steam cylinders driving the rear axle, they could hear running water all around them now above the less violent snapping of the brush they were busting through. He peered over the side. He didn't like the looks of the brown sheet whipping under the running board or through the wheel spokes.

"We're not going to make it much farther," he told her. "If we don't turn back now, we might not make it at all."

As she turned around, the water now almost hubcap deep again and moving fast enough to argue with her steering wheel, Stringer reached in the back for his Winchester, aimed it up at the blue sky and began to fire bursts of three until he'd emptied the magazine. Kathy waited until her ears stopped ringing before she challenged, "I give up. I know what Jack London thinks of the Yellow Peril. But I didn't think the Japanese Empire had a war fleet of flying machines yet."

He explained. "Hearing distress signals from the distance might inspire folk to take a look outside before they find themselves floating to Salton's Sink, house and all. It was the least I could do. I reckon it's everyone for themselves now, and . . . Jesus H. Christ, where is all this water coming from!"

Kathy opened her throttle wider. They lit out to the

west, hopefully out of the path of the flood, and made it at last. As they reached dry ground she swung back toward the railroad line, saying, "That was fun. Now we have to go back to that work camp and pick up some more boiler water. We started out on less than we should and . . ."

"Water?" he cried, waving back the way they'd just come.

Kathy explained, "It has to be distilled water, or at least clean enough to drink, dear. Otherwise my itsy-bitsy steam valves get too sticky-icky to do whatever steam valves are supposed to do."

Stringer made a wry face. "Cut the baby talk and drive due south. That ought to take us as close to that construction camp as we want to get until we find out if it's still there."

So she cranked her big stiff steering wheel in a show of muscle which might surprise anyone who'd never made love to her and proceeded to raise dust and flatten brush in that direction.

Had not the steam drive been so silent, Stringer's sharp ears never would have picked up the faint cries off to their left. At first he dismissed it as a bird call. But then he realized he'd never heard a bird call out for help in Spanish, so he told Kathy to halt. Once she'd stopped splintering greasewood, she could hear it too.

"Wait here," Stringer said. "This is no time to bog down, and you're sure to if you stop over there where the water's running."

Without waiting for an answer he rolled out his side and passed around the hood to make for the source of the odd wails. He couldn't see anything ahead but mile after mile of greasewood, swaying like hell now as the water tore through the lower stems. The brush had hidden the water from sight when they were in the car, but now Stringer discovered it was already ankle-deep and warm as spit after spreading over so much sun-baked desert soil.

He called out, *"A 'onde esta, señorita?"* as the water got deeper with every step. A weaker voice called back, *"Aqui! Precipitar por favor!"* Then he got his bearings and hurried toward her as she'd pleaded with him to hurry.

The Mexican girl, if she was a Mexican girl under all that muck, lay on her side in six inches of muddy water, propped up on one elbow with her left leg pinned under her fallen pony. The pony hadn't made out so well. Its muzzle was under the swirling brown water and, like its rider, it was caked all over with slimy mud. Stringer grabbed the horn of her saddle, planted both boot heels in the muck, took a deep breath and grunted, *"Ahora!"* as he lifted the pony as much as he could.

She had enough spunk to try to work her way out from under the dead animal. Still, it still took them over a dozen tries, working together, and in the end she lost her left boot. By this time she'd figured out what, if not who, Stringer was. So, as he hauled her to her feet in the now shin-deep current, she cried out in pretty good English, "Forget the boot. Where . . . oh where is the nearest dry ground?"

"Too far for you to make it half barefoot," he said as he scooped her up in his arms.

The girl worried, "Oh, I am getting you all muddy!" But Stringer brushed aside her protests as he started wading with her back to Kathy and the steamer.

By the time they reached the car, they had established who he was and that she was Maria Herrerra, who vaguely recalled a Juan Donovan, but hadn't seen him recently and who was a lot more worried about her parents and the others who'd lit out from her spread on horseback when the dooryard suddenly turned into a frog pond in the middle of the desert. Her own pony had bolted with her when it found its hooves coming down in fetlock-deep goo. Then it had fallen with her, as Stringer already knew, and managed to drown itself in just a few inches of water and a heap of blind panic. She didn't know where the others were and prayed they had made it.

He assured her they were heading for the only high ground for miles and that anyone else with a lick of sense ought to wind up atop the railroad bank sooner or later.

When Kathy Doyle saw them coming she quickly hauled out a wool blanket to wrap around the sopping wet little gal. When Maria protested she didn't want to ruin La Señora's blanket, Kathy told her to shut up and asked Stringer to put her in the back, which he did, tucking the blanket securely around the wet and unhappy girl. Then they were off and running for the railroad once more. As the Stanley fought its way up the slope a few minutes later it failed to put as much muscle into the effort as before. And when the front wheels got to the first rail, the Stanley gasped its last.

"Well," Kathy announced, "that's that. We'll have to walk the rest of the way and bring back fresh boiler water from the camp."

Then, as she stood up to step down, Kathy got her first clear look at what had been the desert south of the tracks. "Good heavens," she exclaimed, "we've just discovered a whole new ocean!"

Stringer got out on his side and strode across the tracks to stop and stare increduously at what seemed to be a greasewood-studded sea, though maybe swamp would better describe it, all the way to the southern horizon. It seemed no more than a foot or so deep in any one spot, but that still added up to a fantastic amount of water.

He rejoined the girls to inform them, "The culverts under this railbed can't drain all that water north as fast it seems to keep coming. Don't ask me where it's coming from. This has to be the flood of the century, new as this century may be!"

He was right, although neither he nor anyone else could see the whole picture at that point. Days later they would learn how most of the time, even in flood, the muddy Colorado picked up the lesser currents of the Gila to keep trending seaward between low muddy banks. Failing that, the Colorado spread out across empty miles of its lower delta. But this hadn't been most of the time. The Colorado had made its way sedately enough to just above Yuma, only slightly swollen by early snow melt and thus still within its banks. But the recent late winter rains had fallen unusually hard on the upper watersheds of the Gila and its tributaries, turning that normally placid river into a snarling wolverine of brawling brown foam that played hell with its banks as it tore west across the Arizona desert at express train speed.

Hitting the already high Colorado, all that water had no place to go but up over the west banks and across the flatter desert in that direction, searching for a channel, any channel, to do what water did naturally, namely run downhill. The wide wall of water found a weak spot at a temporary floodgate, designed to control one hell of a lot less water, and smashed through to flood the incomplete southern diversion. And then, the pent-up water found its way to its old bed along the fossil Alamo channel to Salton's Sink and piled against the railroad bank blocking its downhill course to below sea level. Even as Stringer watched, although he couldn't see it yet, the wide sheet of floodwater had reached Salton's Sink to do two awesome things at once.

Salton's Sink was already filling with water, forming a vast inland lake, or salt lagoon. Meanwhile, the somewhat softer silt of the long-gone Alamo River was being cleaned out by the swift currents choosing it as the main course. It would take some time for anyone but lizards to notice, but as the old river bed was being scoured out, a twenty-foot waterfall was moving back up the reborn river about as fast as a human walked. The result was more than just a terribly destructive flash flood. The mighty Colorado was changing its course. Unless someone did something about it fast, the combined waters of the Colorado and all its many tributaries would run down into the Imperial Valley and just keep running until, in years to come, the desert as far north as Indio would be a huge and useless sea, far saltier than any ocean.

But as Stringer and the girls watched in wonder, only grasping a small part of the bigger picture, the vast shallow sea of floodwater that was still impounded by the railroad embankment kept getting even deeper until, as if tired of screwing around with all those puny gushing culverts, the reborn desert river simply balled up a big wet fist and punched its way through in a house-high wall of swirling wet wreckage.

CHAPTER
TWELVE

"Good God!" gasped Kathy Doyle as the ground began to tremble under their feet. "I think we're having an earthquake!"

But as Stringer heard the thunder rolling their way, he declared, "I sure wish it was just an earthquake. It sounds more like this railroad's gone out of business to the east and . . . Jumping Jesus, there she blows!"

As the three of them stared in stunned dismay they could see tiny human figures down the tracks, heading their way as if the hounds of hell were chasing them. Hell it certainly was, in the form of churning brown water that swept away its pitiful human victims in a meat grinder of churning mud, railroad ballast rocks, and cross-ties flipping end over end as the water burst through the gap in the railroad bank to tear northward into Salton's Sink at forty to sixty miles an hour. The water and all the wreckage in its muddy embrace ran fastest where the current was already braiding deeper channels across the hitherto flat desert floor. The silt of the big valley, water-deposited to begin with, cut like brown sugar exposed to the slanting stream of a gigantic fire hose. Behind Stringer and Kathy the blanket-wrapped Maria made the sign of the cross and sobbed, "Oh, my poor little casa!"

Neither of her American rescuers could make out where, amid all that spreading devastation one particular roof top might have been. As a tiny human figure was whipped atop a spreading wave and flipped twice, limply, in the air beyond, Kathy gasped, "Oh, no, that looked like a child!"

Stringer didn't answer. Then a bigger body, in a torn dress, made the same grotesque dolphin jump to vanish just as quickly under the muddy surface again, and Kathy made the sign of the cross as well.

She screamed, "We can't just stand here! We have to do something!"

Stringer tried to calm her. "Let's not panic," he declared, as he searched about for a place to start running for. The desert floor was still dry to the north, and on the far side, to the south, the wide shallow sea they'd just noticed seemed to be turning into a big muddy swamp as the Colorado receded, or at least cut itself a new channel. Farther east, along the track, he saw the survivors were no longer running.

"The gap doesn't seem to be spreading any wider," he told the girls. "I guess the river thinks it's wide enough."

"I hope so. What do we do now?" Kathy asked him.

"For openers you'd best break out a water can and carry it down to that swamp." Stringer took off both his hat and sateen bandana and handed them to her. "If you can use my hat to bail water and screen it through this close-meshed sateen, you ought to wind up with boiler water that'll just have to do. Any fresh water those others still have right now are for human gizzards alone."

She protested, "Where will you be while I do all the work?"

He pointed down the track and explained grimly. "Yonder. I know we can't carry the whole blamed camp to El Centro in your steamer, but somebody could be more hurt than the others."

Kathy started to ask a dumb question. Then she nodded and said, "Well, anyone can see we can't stay *here*."

Stringer didn't answer. He was already legging it east in his squishy boots. It only took him a few minutes to make the half mile or so. When he got there he found Blacky Burke, Gus, and about two dozen Mexicans staring in awe at the broad brown river pouring through the gap in the railroad bank. When he asked who the others on the far side might be, Burke shrugged and answered, "Your guess is as good as mine. Me and Gus are the only white men who made it out in time this way."

Stringer nodded and called out in Spanish, asking if anyone was hurt. There were over a half dozen customers for Kathy's Stanley steamer, and a couple of badly gashed kids looked as if they'd barely make it. Their mothers, some of them banged up as well, had managed to dress the more serious wounds with torn strips of muddy skirting.

Stringer counted noses and impatiently shushed the babble. *"Bueno.* If the able-bodied will help me get the injured to that white horseless carriage you can see up the tracks to the west, the gringa who owns it may have just enough room to get at least the more badly hurt to the doctors in El Centro. Now, vamanos!"

Burke and Gus were the only men there who didn't

offer help as Stringer led the pitiful group toward Kathy's Stanley, carrying a baby in his arms and leading a little girl with a gashed forehead. As they all got close enough to make out details Stringer saw that Maria had brushed off most of the mud which had dried by now and had thrown the blanket aside as the desert sun got warmer. She was a lot prettier than he'd imagined, even with her hair still a mess and her riding skirt torn up one side to expose some mighty shapely thigh.

Both girls moved to meet them. Maria took the baby from Stringer, cooing at it like a desert dove, while Kathy picked up the little girl, calling her a poor dear and setting her in the back seat atop their gear. As she fussed over the child, she told Stringer, "I filled the boiler. Don't ask me with what. It smells just awful."

He told her it ought to get them at least as far as El Centro and added, "You can't miss it if you just follow the tracks to the southwest. On the dry side, of course."

As Maria helped a fat Mexican woman with one arm in a sling into the back beside the little girl, Kathy anxiously asked Stringer why he needed to give her directions. "Aren't you coming with us, for heaven's sake?" she cried, as he shook his head and started to explain.

Then someone gasped, *"Mira!"* and they all turned to see Cactus Jack Donovan or his mud-caked ghost floundering up the bank from the south, gasping, cussing, and sort of sobbing to himself. As one of the Mexicans helped him up to the flatter surface Cactus Jack spotted Stringer in the crowd and blurted, "I lost my pony out yonder. Lord knows how I ever made it. I didn't know I could swim. The folks I rode out to warn had already cleared out by the time I got there. The water was over their doorsill by then. But as I was headed back I saw more water coming at me than I ever want to see again. It come in one big wave, saddle-horn high and studded with tore-up sticker bush. We tried to outrun it, but it caught up with us and the next I knew me and my poor pony was going ass over tea kettle for a million wet years. I don't know where my pony wound up. All I know is I come to be hung up to dry in a greasewood clump along the shallows of that infernal deluge. Do you reckon my Maria and her folk made it?"

Stringer was about to give him the good news when Blacky Burke bulled through the crowd to join them. "You got back just in time, you love-sick cuss. We were just fixing to light out for town in this here horseless carriage."

Stringer shook his head. "Not hardly. There's barely room for the injured. Us able-bodied men have to stay put here until help from the outside world arrives."

Burke snapped, "The hell you say. The trackside wires are torn out for at least a mile, and trains don't run when the wires are down. We can't just stay out here with no food and water. And even if we could, I don't aim to. I'm still in charge of this outfit."

"That's right," growled the nearby Gus, making a meaningful adjustment to his gunbelt, as Stringer weighed the odds. He didn't like them, but he didn't fool with his own gunbelt. He'd been raised to leave his gun alone unless he meant to draw it. He took a deep breath, let half of it out to keep his voice firm, and said, "We got plenty of water out here now, thanks to you boys, and I fail to see any outfit anymores for anyone to be in charge of it. You screwed things up by the numbers, Blacky. It's about time to start doing things sensible for a change, and anyone can see these folk you've banged up and damn near drowned need doctoring more than you or me."

Burke smiled thinly, shot a meaningful glance each

way to include his two hired gunmen, and asked Stringer, "Would you like to bet on that?"

Stringer took a step backwards to get them all in view at the same time as he replied softly, "If I have to."

Blacky had just replied, "You have to," when Maria Herrerra got out of the Stanley steamer, calling out, "El Señor is right! Nobody who is not badly hurt should take up room in this machine. I am staying here as well!"

Cactus Jack's jaw dropped, even as Blacky Burke, oblivious to what he must have taken as more Spanish she-male chatter, went for his six-gun!

Stringer beat him to the draw, just barely, and knew even as he aimed at Blacky that both Gus and Cactus Jack had their own guns clear of leather. But as the shot Stringer put into Blacky's chest was followed a split second later by the roar of Cactus Jack's big .45, it was Gus, not himself, that staggered backwards.

Stringer still dropped to one side and covered Cactus Jack as the gunsmoke from the close quarter's fight hung misty above the tracks. Then Stringer saw Gus had rolled down the far side into the mud, Blacky Burke lay flat on his back between the eastbound tracks, and Cactus Jack had lowered the smoking muzzle of his .45 to stare in moon-struck admiration at the spunky Maria, declaring, "Tell her how glad I am to see her alive, MacEwen."

Stringer didn't have to. Maria shyly told the mud-covered lout to speak for himself, adding, "You were most brave just now, Señor Juan. I confess I thought you were one of those most wicked men until the last moment!"

Cactus Jack scuffed at the railroad ballast with an awkward toe and put his warm .45 away as he answered soberly, "So did they, I reckon. I sure can't say I was brung up no angel, Miss Maria, but anyone can see old MacEwen here had the right notion."

Stringer got back to his feet, reloading the spent chamber of his .38 as he grinned. "Welcome to the human race, Jack. You had me worried there for a moment."

The man who'd no doubt murdered Herbert Lockwood in cold blood shrugged. "There's limits to what any man who shaves with a mirror can abide. What say we get these sick folk on their way, now?"

Stringer agreed and pushed through the crowd to where an ashen-faced Kathy Doyle sat behind the wheel of her overloaded steamer.

"I'd like my hat and bandana back now, honey," he told her. "If this critter can run less'n fifty miles on stinky and no-doubt alkali water, you ought to make it in less than three hours. I'd ask you to wire my story in for me as well, but considering past and future favors let's just say adios and hope you don't get stuck in the desert."

She nodded and told everyone to stand back as she threw her overloaded machine in reverse and tore backwards off the railroad bank amid clouds of dust and considerable screams of terror from her passengers. As she spun around to go crashing west in an even higher cloud of dust, Stringer chuckled and asked Maria and Cactus Jack, "Ain't she the bee's knees? I don't think she knows how to drive that thing slow."

"She sure steers it good fast," Cactus Jack replied. "What was that about her wiring a story for you, MacEwen? I couldn't help overhearing."

Stringer said, "My name's not MacEwen. It's MacKail, Stringer MacKail. I'm not a gunslick. I'm a newspaperman, just like she is, save for her skirts."

Cactus Jack laughed incredulously. "Do tell? Well I'll

be swanned. Blacky had me looking to gun you if ever you showed up."

Maria said firmly, "Don't you dare, Juan! El Señor is the one who saved me from drowning out there on the flooded flats!"

Cactus Jack nodded shyly as he replied, "I just said as much, little darling. But I'm sure glad to know I had even more call to help him just now." Then he turned back to Stringer, asking, "What do you want us to do now, seeing you seem to be the one in charge here, pard?"

It was a good question, and Stringer could see that almost a dozen Mexican men and a couple more brave mujeres expected him to answer it.

"Well," he said, "we'd best all move back to see if anything at all may be left of that camp. There could be some supplies that weren't swept through when the bank gave way betwixt the culverts. I'm afraid your late boss was right about the wires being down. Any trains coming will be coming mighty slow and thoughtful, if at all. We're more likely to die of cholera than thirst unless we boil any of that water we drink. Food will be our big problem, followed by shade. So let's see what we can work out."

One of the workers asked what Stringer wanted to do about Burke's remains. When Stringer said he didn't care, a trio of them lagged behind to help themselves to the dead man's valuables before they rolled him over the side to sprawl in the muck with old Gus.

CHAPTER
THIRTEEN

It was late afternoon when the Southern Pacific Special ordered out of the L. A. yards by Mister Henry Huntington in the flesh nosed to a cautious stop near the brand-new and very inconvenient channel of the Colorado River.

As the middle-aged railroad magnate climbed stiffly down from his private car near the rear of the Special to crunch warily up the north and therefore westbound tracks, he told one of the lackies with him, "It seems to be true. How long do our slide-rule boys say it will take to fill up the whole damned basin, Roy?"

The yes-man replied soberly, "Two or three years, sir. The river doesn't carry half as much water most of the year."

Huntington paused to stare northwards. He wasn't sure whether it was a mirage or a distant blue lake he was gazing at on the horizon. He grimaced, then demanded, "No chance of the river returning to its old bed, once this high water goes down?"

Another member of his party, dressed in riding britches and laced boots, and hence less required to fawn, answered him. "Not now, H. E. Yuma reports, the long way around, that once the current to the gulf reversed, the flood waters dropped tons of silt to dam the old channel. Now that it has a way to run deeper than sea level, I can't see it trying to cut its way through those sea level and mudflats to the south."

Huntington grumbled. "All right. Let's move on up and see what we're talking about."

As the modest trainload of S. P. dignitaries moved on down the line they soon encountered Stringer and his bedraggled followers camped under improvised tents with greasewood cook fires burning between the tracks.

H. E. Huntington strode forward with his silver-handled cane, pointing its tip at the nearest fire as he met Stringer and demanding, "What do you mean by camping on my railroad's right of way, young sir?"

Stringer replied directly, "We had to. It's the only solid camping ground in these parts. I'm Stringer MacKail from the *San Francisco Sun*. These other folk are the survivors of the construction camp that used to be around here somewhere. Some of 'em waded across from the far tracks once the water settled down."

The railroad magnate turned to his field engineer and said, "Make a note of that, Hoover. The channel isn't as deep as it may look. I just wish it wasn't so damned wide. Do you think we can drive piles that might stay put?"

The younger man called Hoover nodded dubiously and replied, "A causeway on piles will surely cost less than a bridge span that wide, H. E. Of course, we'll want to drop some rip-rap just downstream to slow the current, but . . ."

"Don't you mean upstream?" demanded his boss, who seemed to feel he knew everything.

The engineer shook his head. "No, sir. You want to back the current under the piles and let the mud in that soupy current settle, not scour deeper."

Stringer interrupted this exchange. "This is all mighty interesting, gents, but I got some folk here who haven't had a square meal all day. We could all use a ride back to at least as far as El Centro too."

The big boss shot an impatient glance past Stringer, softened when he saw how bedraggled they all looked, and nodded curtly. "Of course. My help will see to feeding everyone from my kitchen car, and naturally we can't leave you here as we consider our options. I'm Henry E. Huntington by the way."

Stringer nodded in response. "I figured you might be."

Then he waved Cactus Jack over and told him, "Have our refugees toss all that stuff off the tracks and make sure the fires are out for good. Then herd 'em all back to wherever Mister Huntington here wants 'em. We're getting out of here after all, courtesy of the Southern Pacific."

Cactus Jack looked dubious as he replied, "I was told never to look a gift whore in the mouth. But my grand-children will never believe me and Maria was saved by the Octopus!"

Huntington cursed under his breath and ordered one of his yes-men to go with Cactus Jack and see to it. As they moved away, he growled, "I wish I could get my hands on that damned Frank Norris! He had no right to stick us with that libelous nickname!"

Stringer replied casually, "The Battle of Mussel Slough was before my time, Hank. I'll take your word the S. P. hasn't out and out murdered anyone since your uncle, Creep Huntington, passed his railroad down to you."

The surviving member of the Huntington clan muttered sarcastically, "Oh, thank you very much. Now, suppose you tell me who I have to thank for tearing out the mile or so of my main line across this damned desert!"

Stringer said, "Your own water outfit, Hank. They were running the water too far north in spite of the warnings of a hydraulic engineer who knew better. That sort of tree stump sticking up out of the mud yonder is what's left to show of the steam shovel you lost as well digging the waterway straight and careless too close to your tracks."

Huntington looked indignant and demanded, "Where do you get off accusing me or my railroad of digging anything, goddamn it? That water syndicate was irrigating this valley on its own, you idiot!"

Stringer cocked an eyebrow as he replied. "Do tell? Seems to me you and your S. P. land office was selling off a heap of fine new irrigated or soon to be irrigated land in these part, Hank."

Huntington snapped, "Of course we sold off all the old land grants around here that we could. What would you do with desert land that could be irrigated, pay the damned taxes on it in hopes of a better deal?" Then he added, "I'm not used to being addressed as Hank, by the way. I'm not sure I like your attitude, young sir."

Stringer noticed some of the others were trying not to grin back at him as he replied dryly, "It's a good thing I don't work for you then, right? You know what everyone's going to say about this mess once it gets out, don't you?"

Huntington shrugged. "They'll no doubt describe it as one hell of a mess. At least for once nobody can pin anything from an earthquake to a falling redwood on the poor old Southern Pacific!"

Stringer asked, "Want to bet? More folk have read that novel by Frank Norris than your railroad has ever given one ride to. I mean to check out your denial that we don't have the Octopus to thank for the inland sea California seems to be sprouting as we stand here. If it's true nobody working for you caused this more recent disaster, I'll be proud to say so when I write the story for the *Sun*. Whether anyone will buy it is sort up for grabs. You and your railroad have an awful reputation to live down, Hank."

Huntington almost groaned as he sadly replied, "I know that all too well, damn it. But what can I do about the business methods of my dead uncle? He didn't do half the mean things he was accused of, and I can't seem to convince anyone the S. P. is under new management. I've been trying to get along with everyone better, but every time some hobo falls off one of our box cars half the papers in California chalk him up as yet another innocent victim of the . . . well, you know."

"Octopus," Stringer replied flatly. Then he added, "I've heard of the charity work your lady does, Hank. I know you collect fine art and even let folk in free to look at it, when you feel up to company. But whether the one and original C. P. Huntington did half the things they say he did or was only bragging, you do have some family skeletons to live down, don't you?"

Huntington's shoulders sagged as he sighed. "That's for damned sure. But you say you'll report this mess out here the way it really happened, with no remarks about aquatic life forms?"

Stringer nodded, but pointed east at the rolling brown water running down into poor little Juanita's ghost sea. "Southern California is surely going to demand a villain to blame all this on. No offense, but you and your S. P. have a head start. That big basin to the north isn't just going to fill to sea level and then stop. It figures to keep filling, and filling some more, until such time as it gets to slop over the other way and head for the sea once more by way of any channel it feels like cutting."

Huntington grimaced and turned questioningly to his nearby engineer. "Hoover?"

The engineer replied with a morose nod, "He's right, H. E. Of course, we're talking about at least some years in the future. That's one hell of an inland sea to fill all the way to the brim with fresh water, given the yearly flow of the Gila-Colorado system."

Stringer pointed out, "The resulting lake won't be fresh at all. It's sure to soak up all the salt left by the fossil sea that used to be there. As it climbs higher each year it will drown out all the crop lands you and others have already sold a heap of suckers, Hank. Meanwhile, the Mexican farmers who used to depend on fresh river water below Yuma and the nearby border won't have any water at all. Ah, do you reckon that book by Frank Norris has been translated into Spanish yet?"

"If it hasn't, I can see it soon will be," Huntington groaned. "You don't have to tell me about the human yen for easy villains. But didn't you just say it was the men running the water syndicate who made this terrible misjudgment?"

Stringer nodded. "The field supervisor who really done this part of the deed is dead. He was cutting corners for a bonus against any instructions the big shots in Yuma might have fed him. So no matter what they told him to do, they're sure to insist it wasn't their fault, and none of them are half as famous, or notorious, as you, Hank."

Huntington groaned again. "Just what I want to hear.

At least a few years of constant complaints and so-called exposé articles about the way I turned most of the Imperial Valley into a great, big, useless, salty mud puddle! But what in the hell do you expect me to do about a mistake I never made, damn it!"

Stringer laughed. "You just answered yourself, Hank. Solve the problem by *damming* it. You have to replace your tracks out here in any case. How much more will it cost you to dam the new channel with a causeway dam instead of a skimpy bridge on piles?"

Huntington frowned at the now quieter but impressive river running north across his right of way and demanded, "Hoover?"

The engineer answered, "A lot, sir. That's a wicked current, and should the waters rise again before we can fill such a broad channel in with coffer dams and rip-rap all bets are off. I'd have to work out the details with my staff, of course, but as a conservative estimate, I can promise you that a causeway on piles, allowing the water to pass on through, would cost you less than a tenth as much."

Stringer's heart sank as he saw the cash-register tags click up and down in the railroad magnate's shrewd eyes. He tried again. "What about the settlers you've already sold land to? Land you know damn well figures to wind up under salty water?"

Huntington shrugged in reply. "I don't own or pay taxes on land I no longer own. I understand the value of good public relations as well as anyone, young sir. God knows I've spent enough of it trying to make the peasants show just a little more respect to me and mine, for all the good it's done. I even gave a public park to Pasadena and the ruffians still hiss at my poor wife when she drives by it!"

Stringer said, "Some folk are like that when they see

a fancy carriage, no matter who might be riding in it, Hank. Playing Lord and Lady Bountiful is one thing. You have a chance right here to be a hero. All the farm folk you save will never forget you—*if* you save 'em that is. How much can one little dam cost, next to that "Blueboy" on the wall of your big house in Pasadena?"

Huntington didn't have to turn to his engineer to answer that one. "One hell of a lot more," he snapped. "We're not talking about a 'little dam,' you idiot. Look at that damned river out there now. You expect me to dam the waters of the Gila and Colorado combined, just to get in good with the neighbors?"

Stringer tried to make his shrug look as if he didn't care. "I would, if I had half your money and gave two hoots and a holler about my neighbors. Whether you like folk or not, Hank, this is your chance to make up for all the mean things the Southern Pacific ever did to anyone. Can't you see how it would spin old Creep Huntington in his grave if the awful Octopus he set up wound up as the knight in shining armor who saved the whole Imperial Valley, out of the goodness of its hitherto miserly heart?"

Huntington turned away from the depressing view of brown water rolling past, fast and no doubt just as stubborn as his late greedy uncle. Instead of answering Stringer, he just commented, "We'd best all get back aboard and back off now. We've seen the damage. It's worse than I thought, but Hoover here will have to work out some procedures before we do anything about it."

Stringer pressed him for a direct reply. "I wasn't planning on spending the night out here, Hank. So what's it going to be, a solid dam or a leaky causeway? My readers might want to know whether there's to be farm land or a seashore here. In case they want to take up plowing or sail-boating on what surely won't be much of a desert any more!"

Huntington said he had to think about it.

Stringer knew that was the polite way such big shots usually said no.

CHAPTER
FOURTEEN

The Hungtington Special was already bound back to the L. A. yards. Nobody had actually been thrown off at El Centro, but that was where Stringer and the other survivors wound up anyway. The Mexicans, including Maria Herrerra, were anxious for further news about their kith and kin. Cactus Jack was anxious to be near Maria. And Stringer had to offer at least some explanation of his shoot-out in the desert to the county authorities before they heard some Mex singing a corrido about it and put out a fugitive warrant on him.

Stringer and Cactus Jack agreed it would look better if he took the credit, or blame, for both Blacky and Gus, lest the county coroner fear Cactus Jack was making a habit of "fair fights" within local juristiction. Stringer waited until his fellow survivors were set up in town, whether visiting injured relatives or just glad to be safe at last, before he recruited a pair of sensible Mex witnesses who seemed to be on his side. He left Cactus Jack to comfort Maria and led his witnesses to the dinky county courthouse, braced for a grilling on the killing of Blacky and Gus.

The hearing, before one of the coroner's clerks in a side room, was perfunctory and anticlimactical. The big flood had swamped the local authorities' ability to deal with more than one disaster at a time. The clerk listened only a few minutes and never questioned Stringer's witnesses before he confided, "I thank you for reporting two more flood casualties to me, Mister MacKail. But wouldn't it save us all a lot of trouble if we just wrote those rascals off as drowned, along with all the others? Nobody liked either one of 'em, you know, and I'll take your word you gunned them fair in self-defense if you'll take my word they were victims of the deluge."

Stringer protested mildly. "Far be it from me to tell Imperial County how to keep its books. But the last I saw of their cadavers, each had a bullet hole in it."

The assistant coroner shrugged. "By the time all the bodies are gathered for mass burial in this heat, if we ever find them all, who's going to notice? I'll explain it off-the-record to anyone important who might ask. I doubt anyone will. Gus Mason was a known paid assassin and everyone knew he was working for Burke. It was just one of those things that's more easy to know than to prove in court. Both the sheriff and district attorney will be pleased to hear the sons of bitches are no longer a threat to local law and order. But, naturally, it wouldn't look tidy if they congratulated anyone in particular for exterminating such vermin. So why don't you just forget it, and the county will say no more about it."

Stringer agreed that sounded more than fair. So they shook on it, and he took his witnesses across the street and bought them drinks by way of an apology for wasting their time. Each in turn insisted on springing for the next round. So three drinks and almost forty minutes after squaring things with the county Stringer was free to get down to more serious business.

At the Western Union office down the way the clerk on duty said he did, indeed, recall a Miss Kathy Doyle of the *San Francisco Examiner* sending quite a long wire, at day rates, to San Francisco.

"It was a good thing she got here first," he added. "We've been busy as hell ever since, what with all the messages coming in or going out. That flood out in the desert must be a pisser. They've even wired Sacramento to send in the National Guard. Looters from both sides of the border figure to get here before any troops can, right?"

Stringer nodded absently and asked if the clerk was sure Miss Doyle had wired the first flash to nobody else but her own paper. The clerk nodded. "I am. Her message was too long and complicated for me to recall worth mention, even if company policy allowed me to tell one customer just what another one might have sent. I can tell you she only sent the one long wire, though. Was she supposed to send more than one?"

Stringer sighed. "Not really. I knew better, but I had more important matters than my job to worry about. I don't suppose you have any messages from my paper to me?"

The clerk said he sure did and handed three envelopes across the counter. Sam Barca had sent all three at ever-shorter intervals, no doubt after reading the headlines of the goddamned *Examiner*. Only the first could be taken as sardonic. It read, "SO MUCH FOR FLOOD STOP COULD YOU AT LEAST SEND FOLLOW UP WITH ANGLE SOMEONE ELSE MAY NOT HAVE QUESTION MARK BARCA."

The second message thanked him for scooping the rival papers on the public statement issued from Yuma by the Imperial Valley Improvement Company, as the water trust was now calling itself with no mention of water. The third confirmed the Guard had been called out and pleaded with him to at least dig up some local color for "Deleted by Western Union," if he was still alive and thought it at all possible he was still writing for the *Sun*.

Stringer picked up a yellow telegram blank and wrote, "IN EL CENTRO INTERVIEWING LOCALS STOP MORE WHEN NEWSWORTHY STOP" and asked the clerk to get that right off. Then he went out to get back on the job.

He had to pick up another notebook at the general store well before sundown for taking down the tales he heard even using his tight reporter's shorthand. There were many personal stories indeed, each in itself a worthy subject for an adventure novel, whether they'd ever run as a news paragraph or not. For minute by minute the transient population of El Centro kept growing as refugees streamed in to the nearest shelter. Stringer set up shop on the steps of the dinky saloon nearest the railroad platform and took notes as the survivors straggled in. Some were in good shape. Others looked as if they'd been hauled through the keyhole backwards. Stringer didn't pester the ones who seemed just too stunned to feel like talking or even stopping. He offered a helpful service of his own by directing them to the clinic the local doctors, working together as an emergency team, had set up in the shade of the trees where Juanita's gypsy cart had stood what now seemed so long ago. Most of the injuries were cuts and bruises, but swimming in even knee-deep water that was more a greasewood and lumber chowder could tear one up considerable. Those caught by the sudden rush of unexpected irrigation who'd actually drowned or bled to death out on the desert could hardly be interviewed. Stringer had to just guess on the numbers, as survivors, spotting a man with a notebook who might actually know something, asked or told him about missing members of their families.

As the big picture slowly emerged from the bits and pieces each survivor could offer, Stringer learned that the first high wall of muddy water had fanned out widely from the break, losing some but not enough of its punch as it roared across the gentle grade, doing more damage by slamming debris into things and then picking up the pieces to use them in turn like a locust swarm of bitty battering rams. Folk caught by the flood crest any distance out from the first breakthrough had found they'd survived by managing to stay on their feet or, better yet, climbing aboard something high and solid. He heard many a tale of those who'd been hit by floating timber, knocked under, and never seen again. Most tragic was the story of a young mother who'd climbed up in a wagon bed with her three kids, only to find the wagon floating fast toward Salton's Sink. Then suddenly, to the horror of a vaquero watching in the lee of an immovable kitchen range, the woman's wagon had been flipped over and then over and over again by the chocolate-colored floodwater.

A late arrival, coming in on a mighty muddy pony, told of being caught way out by water running only inches deep down the steeper slope of the once-extinct inland sea. He told Stringer that Salton's Sink was already a good-sized lake to the north. But his tale was less of a new lake in what had been bare desert less than twenty-four hours before than that of the naked body of a woman, rolling at him like a log in the swift shallow water, that knocked his pony's legs from under it and rolled them both a ways before horse and rider could stagger back to their feet and somehow keep going. When Stringer asked whether the dead woman had been

Anglo or Mex the muddy rider shuddered and replied, "You couldn't tell. Her hair and hide had been sort of sanded off in her travels. I don't want to think about her no more. If I ever in this world find a place to lay my head, I sure hope I don't dream about her coming at me ass over teakettle, with her peeled-off face grinning up at me like that just before she hit us."

Stringer was more cheered when, late in the afternoon, he spied a big tractor bumping over the train tracks at him with a little train of farm wagons trailing behind its slow but powerful wheels. Stringer leaped to his feet with a happy cry as he recognized old W. R. Brown driving the tractor with a not at all displeased expression. The friendly Coopers and some of the other nester families who'd treated him neighborly right after he'd buried Juanita were aboard the overloaded wagons as well.

As they greeted each other like survivors of a battle meeting later in the rear area, W. R. Brown explained dryly, "You told me to act more neighborly. Me and old Cooper had just plowed that extra length of drainage when the canal commenced to run into it like hell. We could see there was way more water than one canal or even a river could hold. So we got cracking, picking neighbors up as we moved to such high ground as there was. It wasn't near high enough. By the time we got in sight of the railroad bank every wagon I was towing was bed deep in the water and trying to float off with the current. But old Betsy here was just too big and heavy and, thank God, strong enough to hold us all together 'til the water put all our wheels back on the ground."

Cooper joined them to catch the last of that and add, "None of us would have made it if it hadn't been for old W. R. and his monster machine. We lost our housing, our crops in the field, and damn near our lives. But every time I look at my wife and family since, nothing else seems to matter."

W. R. said, "There you go. Our land is still there as well." He turned back to Stringer, explaining. "The water had narrowed down to sort of cut a regular channel by the time it got low enough for us to swing west for town. I don't mind saying Old Betsy had a time getting us across that stretch. She was wheel-hub deep and chewing deeper out in the middle, and no mule team could have hauled one wagon through the mudflats spread all about on both sides. That first boiling wave tore all the greasewood and lizards up by the roots and left the land scalped Cheyenne style. Drilling fruit trees in ought to be a heap easier, once we head back to re-build."

Cooper sighed. "If it ain't under water for keeps, you mean. Remember that rider we met out yonder who said Salton's Sink was more like a Salton Sea right now, and still rising?"

W. R. grimaced as he replied, "Hell, don't be so pessimisticated. Desert flash floods always dry up in a few days. By this time tomorrow you'll be bitching about the dust again. Ain't that right, pard?"

Stringer nodded, even though he wasn't at all sure about that. These half-drowned nesters needed food and shelter more than they needed more to worry about. So he told them, "Unless you folk salvaged some tents, you'd best get to looking for some place to stay here in El Centro. When I left my hotel, quite a spell back, they'd already hired out most of the rooms they had and it's been getting more crowded here in El Centro ever since."

W. R. Brown, who seemed to be in charge whether anyone else had anything to say about that or not, turned to call out, "All right, you folk back there. We're moving on just a mite. So all of you hang on tight, hear?"

Stringer waited until the improvised trackless train passed on, waving back to the one little girl who waved at him, and then he seated himself to write their desert saga down in shorthand while it was fresh in his memory. It was nice to report a bright spot amid all this tragedy. For it was a tragedy, whether or not the survivors themselves were injured in mind and body. Even if the new Salton Sea was stopped no higher than that fossil beach out yonder, rebuilding figured to be a heartbreaking and bankroll-busting task. If the now briny water rose much higher, of course, the settlers north of the tracks at the very least would be ruined. Those who'd bought sections south of the tracks had nothing to feel smug about either if the Colorado started searching for another outlet once it filled everything below sea level to the brim.

Huntington's engineer had said he figured it would take at least a few years for the rogue river to fill the basin to the north. That might mean time to work out a new channel or even get the Colorado back in its own channel, given time, determination, and above all money. If all the threatened settlers, the water trust, the railroad, and mayhaps the government got right at it and soon, there was an outside chance of snatching success out of this disaster. But to date the flood victims were still stunned, the National Guard was more interested in shooting looters than ditch digging, and both the railroad and the water trust were issuing statements denying any responsibility for this act of God, as they'd likely wind up calling human error.

Stringer took his notes inside the saloon and sat at a table to recompose his news feature, knowing there was no way the *Sun* was going to have space for half the sad tales he'd just heard. One beer and two smokes later he had the draft he meant to wire in. He was just about to rise from the table and go send it when an elderly Hispanic in a torn shirt and muddy pants moved to hover over him and ask, *"Permiso, señor?"*

Stringer told the polite old gent to sit down and name his poison, but added, "I've got just about all the survival stories we could possibly use, sir."

The older man sat across from him to reply. "They told me you were the one who was writing everything down, *señor*. I have no important tale of my own to tell. Through the grace of God most of my family and I we outraced the crest of that flood. But my eldest daughter did not make it out with myself and the others. I thought, since you have been talking to so many others who made it to safety. . ."

Stringer cut in. "This may be a wild guess. But would your name be Herrerra, and are we talking about a young lady called Maria?"

The older man's face lit up and he gasped, *"Si!* Oh, *si, si,* but do not toy with a father's hopes, señor!"

Stringer reassured him. "She's alive and well. I thought I saw a family resemblance."

Herrerra pleaded, "Never mind . . . please, sir, where, oh where is our little Maria?"

"At the Hotel Imperial," Stringer said. "She made it here with me and some friends of mine. We booked her in just down the hall from my room. Come on, I'd better go with you."

He didn't say why he offered to accompany the now-impatient father as he stuffed the notes in a hip pocket and rose, adjusting his gunbelt. Maria's father was packing a .45 Walker Conversion, and while Stringer had warned Cactus Jack to behave himself the erstwhile hired gun hadn't been reformed all that long. But Hispanic fathers could leap to conclusions about whether a *gringo* was behaving himself or not.

When they got to the Hotel Imperial, a rambling two-story structure of timber and 'dobe, Stringer led Maria's father up to her room and knocked on the door. There was no answer. Then old Herrerra tried the latch and, finding it unlocked, opened the door on Maria's empty room.

Stringer didn't think this might be the time to knock on other doors up here along the dark hallway looking for Maria. So he led the now-reworried father back down to the desk to ask if Miss Herrerra might have checked out.

The desk clerk recalled no such incident, but added that since he'd been mighty busy with new arrivals pestering him for rooms he just didn't have to hire, the lady might have just gone out for supper or a stroll.

Stringer turned to Herrerra and said, "There you go. Why don't you just find a seat down here in the lobby and sooner or later Miss Maria ought to turn up."

The older man shook his head gravely. "I must get the good news to the rest of my family. Maria's poor mother has not stopped weeping since last we saw our daughter. We are down near the south end of town, staying with our friends, the Garcias. Maria knows them, of course. Would you be so kind as to tell her where her family is the moment you see her?"

Stringer agreed and heaved a silent sigh of relief as the girl's father left. Then he went back up the stairs, two at a time, to dash down to Cactus Jack Donovan's door and knock on it hard as he called out, "Whether you have company or not, we got to talk, Jack!"

On the far side, a bedspring groaned and Stringer heard spurred boots coming to the door. Cactus Jack opened it to stare out at Stringer sort of owl-eyed, with fire water on his breath. Stringer pushed his way inside and saw to his relief the bed was now unoccupied. He quickly told the gunslick, "Maria's father is in town, looking for her. She's not in her room."

Cactus Jack almost sobbed as he told Stringer his sad tale. "She's mad at me. She said she liked me but that she admired some other son of a bitch better and didn't want me kissing her. But you know how gals always say no when they mean yes, so I kissed her anyway and then she slapped me and run out crying. You say old Herrerra's in town, pard? Well, then, point me at him so's I can tell him I mean to marry up with his daughter. You was right about it being better to talk to a Mex gal's daddy first."

Stringer shook his head and said, "You're too drunk to go courting, Jack. Whether Maria really loves another or not, her old man's not likely to want a gringo son-in-law with rot-gut on his breath. Why don't you just lie down and sleep it off? Now that things are starting to settle down again you'll have plenty of time to court the little gal of your dreams the right way."

Cactus Jack swayed uncertainly, then said, "I got to go out and track down that other son of a bitch she said she admires more than me. I'll bet he's a sissy Mex who smears perfumed bear grease in his hair."

Stringer looked at him with disgust. Still, he tried to calm the mean drunk. "She might not have anyone else in mind at all. Come morning, you just take a good bath, find yourself a clean shirt, and rub some stink-pretty in your own curly locks before you go making a sap of yourself, Jack." He took the drunken man's arm, turning him around and heading him back to bed.

The wiry and normally agile gunslick started to argue, then stumbled on over to the bed and took a belly-flop across it, suddenly out like a light.

Stringer stared soberly down at him and muttered, "You and old Samson have a lot in common, you murderous cuss. Strong men approach you at their own peril. But you're just mush in the hands of a pretty young gal."

He tried to put Maria Herrerra and her uncouth swain out of his mind as he went back down and headed for the telegraph office, recomposing his news feature mentally. Then he block-lettered half a dozen pages, feeling mighty wistful about the old Remington he'd left up in Frisco. If they ever got a so-called "portable" typewriter down to less than thirty pounds he meant to be the first in line to buy one.

The new telegraph clerk who'd just come on whistled at the length of the message. "At a nickel a word this is sure going to cost your paper, Mister MacKail. You'd save a heap if we sent in at night-letter rates."

Stringer said, "I know. But I get hell from my boss every time I do that. The pressroom is open around the clock, and while I can't call this a scoop at least it's pretty good as a follow-up."

The clerk agreed to get it right out, since the wire traffic was subsiding now that the whole outside world had a handle on the disaster. His cheery observation failed to cheer Stringer worth mention. As he paused to roll a sunset smoke he told himself sternly not to feel so smug about the love-sick Cactus Jack. For who but a total Samson would have trusted that infernal Kathy Doyle, *again*, after she'd already proven herself a career woman who put her own career first no matter how often a man made her come, or leastways got her to say she did. Right now he didn't buy a word she'd ever said.

As he lit up, he heard a train whistle and ambled over to the nearby tracks to watch a troop train roll in. He'd already wired Sam Barca that the National Guard had been called out. All they were doing at the moment was climbing down out of the boxcars and lining up in their blue shirts and khaki britches, nickel-plated bayonets fixed on their bolt-action Krags, for God's sake. Stringer made a wry grimace. One could always tell peacetime military by how spiffy they looked. Not like that time in Cuba. Those poor soldier boys hadn't charged the Dons with nickel-plated bayonets, goddamn it. It made the still-young Stringer feel old as he pulled down the brim of his old Rough Rider hat and headed back to the hotel.

He checked in her room, but Maria Herrerra hadn't returned yet, and he wasn't about to look for her in Donovan's room. It had been a long day, he'd done the best he could by his feature editor. So he headed for his own hired room to call it a day.

That was where he found Maria Herrerra. He almost drew on her as he stepped into the dark room to see her sitting upright on his own bed. She sobbed, "Oh, where have you been all this time! I have been so worried! Your friend tried for to rape me and I had nobody else to turn to!"

Stringer shut the door, sat down beside her, and hauled off his bandana to dab away her tears as he consoled her. "I don't think old Jack meant to scare you that much. He's just sort of crude. But never you mind. I've got good news for you, honey. I just talked to your father. He and your mother and the others made it after all. They're staying at the Garcia's place. Your father told me you knew where that was."

She clapped her small hands together gleefully and replied, *"Es verdad!* It is just a short walk from here, and they are all alive? Oh, I must go to them, muy pronto!"

Stringer agreed and helped her to her feet. "I'd best escort you over," he offered. "The streets outside are crowded with all sorts, including tin soldiers and, no offense, but you're still showing more leg than the average Gibson Girl."

She didn't argue. She just sprang up to go with him, one of her arms linked through his left one. They made it down the dark stairs without incident. But, as they reached the lobby, Cactus Jack Donovan rose ominously from where he'd been half dozing under a potted paper palm to growl, "I knew it! Stand aside, Miss Maria. Me and this back-stabbing Romeo have serious things to settle!"

Stringer shoved Maria to one side and then smiled as sincerely as he could at Cactus Jack. "You got it all wrong, pard. I was just now taking the lady home to her family."

Cactus Jack growled. "After the two of you spending all this time up in your room, you rat? I'll pard you, if you'll just be good enough to fill your fist, you two-faced, lying sweetheart-stealer!"

Stringer tried again. "Simmer down, for Pete's sake. I've always been able to get my own gals. You scared this one and sent her running to my room, where I promise you she found me out on my own business. You're scaring her even more with all this romantic nonsense. There's nothing to fight about, you damned fool!"

Maria sort of whimpered, "Es verdad, Juan. This other man saved me in the desert. I shall always be his friend for saving me. But nothing more. I told you I was fond of a man of my own people. I swear there is nothing like that between this man here and me but my eternal gratitude."

Cactus Jack flexed his fingers stiffly as he snapped, "Is gratitude what you call what you've been giving old Stringer all this time up in his room?"

Maria snapped, *"Idioso!* He just told you I was alone up there! I tell you he has never treated me with anything but the most gallant respect! Can you say the same, you pawing ape?"

Cactus Jack said, "I got nothing further to say to nobody right now."

Stringer stiffened but said softly, "I don't want to fight you. You're drunk and there's nothing to fight about, damn it!"

Maria crossed herself and pleaded, "Oh, no, somebody stop this, por favor!" But the desk clerk had ducked out of sight, and the three of them had the lobby to themselves.

Cactus Jack snarled, "I ain't too drunk to deal with rats like you. So I'm counting to three and then I mean to draw. You just go on and do whatever you have the mind to, you bastard!"

He started counting as Stringer tried to wake up. For the situation struck him nightmarish as well as mighty dumb. He saw it was getting down to him or Cactus Jack now, whether the loco-in-love as well as reverted-to-type killer had saved his life that time or not.

Then, just as Stringer was tensing to draw, a shot rang out from the dark doorway behind Cactus Jack. The startled Stringer instinctively drew and put a round in the drunken brute's chest before the bullet in his back could drop him with a knuckle-white grip on both his holstered six-guns. He already had one drawn as he hit the floor face first and just lay there. So Stringer quickly kicked it across the waxed floor as he trained his own smoking muzzle on the ominously dark front door.

Then Maria was running over to wrap both arms around her father as Herrerra stepped into the light, his own .45 still smoking. He nodded at Stringer and said, "Forgive me if I interferred in a fight you wished for to finish yourself, señor. Pero, the name of my daughter entered into the conversation and you did seem to be taking far too long for to draw."

Stringer nodded, "That's true. Now, Mister Herrerra, get Miss Maria out of here pronto and let me handle things here."

The older Spanish-speaking gent nodded gravely and told Stringer they would always be in his debt. Then he led his daughter outside saying, "Come, my child, this is no place for those of our people to be when the gringo law arrives."

Stringer expected it might not be such a comfortable place for him either, as the county deputy charged in. Stringer was sedately seated in the chair Cactus Jack had vacated, his own gun reloaded and put away. The deputy cautiously approached the body sprawled between them, rolled it over and grunted. "Always knew Cactus Jack would wind up like this sooner or later," he commented. "Might you know the gent he pushed his luck too far with at last?"

"I cannot tell a lie," Stringer confessed. "It was me. I've already explained, over at your courthouse, why I had to shoot it out with the gents he was working for. I thought it was over. I hope it is now."

The deputy straightened up, putting his gun politely away. "I hope so too. Good riddance to bad rubbish. But I reckon we'd best go over and give 'em some sort of statement at least. Then I'd be proud to buy you a drink. How did he start it, this time?"

Stringer got to his feet. "Oh, you know how a gent with a chip on his shoulder and guns on his hips might say just about anything, as long as it's ugly," he explained. "I could say this was sort of an argument over a lady. But since the lady's not here, I won't."

CHAPTER
FIFTEEN

Stringer found himself free to leave town before midnight, but since there wouldn't be another train out before morning he enjoyed the novelty of a good night's sleep between clean sheets, alone, and had a hearty breakfast in the morning.

By the time he was ready to board, the dinky but now overstuffed town of El Centro seemed to have more law and order than it really needed, with a National Guardsman stationed at all the halfway important intersections and a machine-gun set up behind sandbags in front of the bank.

Stringer was unable to verify the rumors about the hanging of at least three looters or a column of Mexican raiders turned back near Calexico, with heavy losses on both sides. He knew from his stint in Cuba as a war correspondent that there seemed to be a latreen orderly posted to every company who was not averse to pulling extra duty as a bullshit artist. So, since the emergency as well as the flood seemed to have passed its crest, he boarded the crowded westbound with his S&W .38 wrapped in its belt inside his battered gladstone.

A few hours later he got off to change trains in L. A., with his gun still in that position. He began to wonder if he might not have been hasty when two moose-like individuals fell in step with him on either side and told him someone wanted to talk to him, right now.

He didn't think it prudent to ask what would happen if he told them to go to hell, so in silence they frog-marched him off the platform, through the waiting room, and into a part of the depot that wasn't open to the general public. Then, as one of them moved ahead to open a door, the other nudged Stringer from behind and commanded him to enter. So he did as he was told, not seeing much alternative.

He was only mildly surprised to find himself facing old H. E. Huntington again. The railroad magnate was seated behind an acre of expensive desk in an oak-paneled office. Through an open archway to his own right, Stringer could see part of a less luxurious layout he took to be a drafting room. At least one draftsman wearing a green eyeshade was in there working a mile a minute at a slanted drafting table.

Stringer nodded down at Huntington. "Howdy, Hank. These apes of yours said you wanted to see me."

Huntington looked as if he was trying to make up his mind whether he wanted to laugh like a hyena or froth at the mouth like a mad dog. In the end he settled for snarling, "You crazy son of a bitch! Who gave you the right to publish that whopper to the effect that the Southern Pacific was already hard at work to dam the rogue Colorado and put it back in its old course?"

Stringer explained, "The *San Francisco Sun* did the publishing. Us writers can only submit stories for publication. You'd be surprised how often they turn us poor working stiffs down. You see, the publisher can even fire the editor so . . ."

"Never mind all that bullshit!" Huntington cut in. "I collect rare books as well as oil paintings and statuary. You were the one who wrote that obscene as well as total lie about our position regarding that damned flood! The Southern Pacific is a railroad, not a water company. We bear no guilt and we don't owe a wooden nickel for the mistakes of others, damn it!"

Stringer nodded agreement. "I know. I put that in my report. Didn't you read the part where I praised you and your engineers for being such swell gents? How often can it be said a big hard-fisted tycoon like you is willing to help the little fellow in such an unselfish way, Hank?"

As he hoped, the nephew of the once-feared and hated Creep Huntington didn't seem to mind being called a big hard-fisted anything. But his voice seemed to soften more than his heart as he insisted, "You're going to have to print a retraction. I told you I'd *think* about it, not that I'd *do* it, you damned troublemaker! My slide-rule boys tell me the job would take two or more years, if we were lucky, and nobody's dared to name a figure as to how much it would cost us!"

Stringer shot a sardonic glance at the nearest hired tough before he shrugged. "Well, far be it from me to refuse to file a story even more exiting than the first one, Hank. I can see the headline now, OCTOPUS BACKS DOWN! That ought to be worth an extra edition, don't you think?"

H. E. Huntington answered flatly. "You print it like that and I swear I'll have your job, if I have to buy your paper outright to enjoy the pleasure of firing you myself!"

Stringer shrugged off these words. "It wouldn't be much pleasure working for you in any case, Hank. But let's say we do it your way, or at least try. Let's say the *Sun* publishes a humble retraction, explaining that a dumb field stringer mistook you for a public-spirited gent in the heat of the moment and allowing its not your fault that all that grant land the S. P. sold to a lot of poor suckers is fixing to slide under the Salton Sea. Let's even quote you to the effect that you've studied how you might have been able to help and that you just decided it was too big a job. Have you ever held a straw out to a drowning man and then snatched it back from him, Hank? We're talking about hundreds of farm folk who figure to lose everything they own. Way more than the number of nesters your uncle screwed in Tulare County during the Mussel Slough incident. That was more than twenty years ago, and by now a whole generation of kids have been raised to spit when they hear the letters S or P."

Huntington looked pained. "I had nothing to do with the so-called Battle of Mussel Slough. I never would have approved it. I know my late uncle could be stubborn when he thought he was in the right, but . . ."

"Just like you." Stringer cut in. "I never settled on uncleared title in Tulare County. So I can see how the Southern Pacific was in the right, from a purely legal standpoint. The little folk who lost land they thought was their own have yet to forgive the Octopus to this day."

"This is different," protested Huntington.

Stringer only nodded pleasantly. "Many a beaten wife would agree its at least a mite different every time she winds up bruised. Let's say we let your own public relations department write up as oily a self-serving retraction as they know how. Let's say I toss in a full apology of my own for misunderstanding your intent. How many California readers are going to take it as anything but another slimy slither of their favorite hate, the one and original Octopus?"

Huntington banged his fist on the desk and roared, "You goddamned country slicker, you knew you'd be putting us in this spot when you wrote that goddamned story, didn't you?"

Stringer grinned sheepishly but not particularly apologetically. "I sure was hoping it would and that you'd be smart enough to see it. You see, I really feel sorry for those nesters in the soon-to-be liquid Colorado Desert, Hank."

Huntington growled, "I ought to have you killed. I would if I thought it would do any good at this late date." Then he rose from his desk and added, "Come on. Maybe this time we can see that you get the story right for a change."

He led Stringer into the nearby drafting room, where Stringer could now see half a dozen men hard at work over drafting tables. A bigger chart table occupied the center of the room. Huntington led Stringer to it and pointed down at the big contour map of the country he'd just visited the hard way.

Huntington said, "The reason I'd sure like to get out of it goes like so." He pointed with a pencil eraser as he continued, "To begin with we have to lay new tracks, this way, to restore cross-country service before the effing Santa Fe takes it away from us. We'd planned on that in any case. My boys tell me we could pile drive a causeway across the running water. They say the river won't mind as long as the piles are well spaced in its bed. That's all it would take to run my trains across on a live-and-let-live basis. But the infernal Mexicans below Yuma are already accusing me—*me* of all people!—of stealing their damned drinking water. The old bed is full of salty tide water all the way north of the border." He snorted in indignation. "How do you say 'octopus' in Spanish?"

Stringer said, *"Pulpo,* I think. I guess they published that book by Frank Norris in at least one Spanish edition after all, Hank."

Huntington swore and said, "I sure wish they hadn't. It hurts enough to be called a greedy squid in your own lingo."

Then he pointed at the old bed of the Alamo, now the new bed of the Colorado, on his big chart and continued. "My boys tell me they can use free brush off the surrounding flats to jam down to the river bed between their piles. That means that every foot or so we narrow the mid-channel, the water figures to rise at least a few inches and move that much faster through the gap. If we wait for slack water after the last spring rains, we may be able to finish our big beaver dam before the next high water. If we get a wet summer . . . well, lots of luck. You could be costing us years of profitless beaver work, Stringer."

The younger man shrugged but looked straight at Huntington. "Wouldn't you rather be called a beaver than an octopus, Hank? You know you can do it, sooner or later, and once you have the Colorado back in its old bed you'll have all that railroad grant land instead of a salt marsh to peddle, once the water syndicate's back in business again, right?"

Huntington looked like he'd just been caught with a hand in the cookie jar as he muttered, "If and when the water trust goes back into business it'll be under new management. Charly Rockford had so many process-servers after him that he filed for bankruptcy and ran for higher ground."

Stringer shot the savior of Southern California a sharp look, adding caustically, "We may have spoken in haste about old Creep Huntington spinning in his grave. How much did it cost you to corner all the shares at say ten cents on the dollar, you sly dog?"

Huntington just smiled. "Well, somebody had to take the fool project in receivership, didn't they? I'll still be surprised as hell if the Southern Pacific breaks even in the end."

Stringer sarcastically agreed. "So will I. Selling water to all those farms and owning the only railroad that can take their produce to market, east or west, is going to be one hell of a cross for you to bear. I take back all I may have said about you being but a puny shadow of the one and original Octopus, Hank. You're a hell of a heap smarter than old Creep, as well."

Huntington grinned like a mean little kid who'd stuck a gal's braid in the ink well and wanted all his classmates to notice. "It's about time I got some respect around here, damn it. Next to being called an octopus, there's nothing that riles me half as much as being called a pale shadow of my less-refined old uncle."

Stringer nodded solemnly. "I promise not to call you a sissy when I report that this time the Southern Pacific is out to save so many little folk instead of screwing 'em. I might even be willing to call you a decent old tough if you'd like to explain how come you just made me sweat so much out front. You knew all the time you meant to go through with damming that rogue river, right?"

Huntington growled at him. "You deserved some

sweating. You made *me* sweat like hell before I could see anything but red on the books of my poor railroad. Now get out of here before you talk me into endowing every brat in California with a damned lollipop, you slick-talking rascal!"

CHAPTER
SIXTEEN

The tedious trip up from L. A. to Frisco on top of the previous day's haul across the desert from El Centro, had more than tired Stringer out. But as he got stiffly down from his Coaster at the Mission Street Station he knew Sam Barca would still be at his news desk.

The day shift was starting to pour out the cast-iron classic front of the mostly brick building when he arrived. He ticked his hat brim to another brace of pretty stenographers and limped inside, crossing the pressroom and dropping his gladstone near the opening of old Sam's frosted glass cage. As he dragged a chair in and sat down, Sam Barca looked up from the copy he was editing. "It's about time you got back," he growled in way of greeting. "Can you verify that last report you filed about the National Guard and those Mex bandits?"

Stringer retorted, "Not hardly. But I figured you wanted all the local color I could come up with."

"Some of the stuff you wrote on the flood victims working together so bravely reads pretty good," Barca

179

admitted grudgingly. "Our readers like to know they're not the only ones who ever offered a helping hand and might not have been suckers after all. I had to cut some of it of course. I sent you to get a story, not to write a novel. But, all right, even if it pains me to say it, you got us a story, indeed."

Stringer tried not to show his surprise at the rare compliment. "Thanks, Sam. I'm sorry the damned *Examiner* scooped us on the first report of the breakthrough. I was dumb enough to trust a woman. So naturally she done me as dirty as usual. I'm glad my follow-up with more details left you in such a good mood."

Sam Barca frowned across the desk at him. "I don't know what you're talking about. How do you figure Kathy Doyle doublecrossed you, as I gather that's who we're talking about."

Stringer frowned back and said, "Hell, Sam, it must have been close to eight hours before I could catch up with her first wire with one of my own. We were both stuck with rescue work first and reporting second. But she was able to get into town way ahead of me and, damn it, don't you even read the headlines of rival papers?"

Barca reached impassively for the pile of earlier editions on a nearby shelf as he muttered, "That's something else we have to talk about." As he handed yesterday's *Sun* across to Stringer he went on, "I had to work out the money with my opposite number at the *Examiner* by telephone. He found it confusing too, since you work for us and she works for them. But the little lady seems to have a will of iron so they agreed, just this once, that as long as they only had to pay her and we had to pay you, both papers could run what you see on page one."

There was more than one story under the screaming headlines about Southern California vanishing under water. When he made out the joint by-lines above the subheading he was searching for, his jaw dropped and he murmured, "Well, I'll be damned." The credit line read, "Exclusive from the Imperial Valley by Miss Kathy Doyle of the *Examiner* and Stringer MacKail of the *San Francisco Sun,* on the scene together when the disaster first began"!

Sam Barca said dryly, "It would have been rude to print our own man's name ahead of a lady's. I thought the two of you wrote it together. What's this stuff about a doublecross?"

Stringer waved him off impatiently. "Hold it, I'm reading!" As he did just that, he could see that Kathy's style was a lot more florid than his own. She'd no doubt felt she needed some phrases Jack London would have been hard put to equal as she described the first horror of that deadly deluge. She got most of the facts right, though, and now that he studied back on it, Maria Herrerra had looked something like "A once-proud member of the Spanish Hidalgo class reduced to a piteous state of mud-plastered hysteria."

Once he'd read it all twice, he gravely handed the paper back to Sam Barca. "Forget what I said about a doublecross. I guess we all live and learn."

Sam Barca replied brusquely, "Let's hope she's learned not to be content with a news break without following up on it. That's all she got on the story, good as it was. I saw no reason to share the scoop you filed on H. E. Huntington, of all people, charging to the rescue. So she's probably sore she didn't stick around, and I'm not at all sure I'm delighted with this sudden change in the public image of the Southern Pacific. I liked it better when they had no redeeming virtues at all. We could always get a Sunday filler out of taking another crack at the ever-evil Octopus. What do you suppose Huntington could be acting so noble for? The S. P. has to be making something on the deal . . . hmmm, that might be worth following up on, right?"

"Wrong," said Stringer. "Old H. E. Huntington may be out to change his public image by doing a good and unselfish deed for a change." Then he added, "And you can't fault any man for that."

Sam Barca muttered, "Shit, I like my big business tycoons just plain down and dirty. I guess we'll have to find another target. How do you feel about Pacific Gas and Electricity? John Muir says they've been treating his pet redwoods mighty awful."

"Not just now, Sam," Stringer protested. "I need a hot tub, a shave, and fresh duds at least as much as anyone needs a redwood tree."

Barca had to agree. "You do look sort of like a cowboy who got bucked off and shit on. Why don't you try to relax and have some innocent fun this coming weekend?"

Stringer swore that he meant to do just that. Then he somewhat spoiled the effect he was trying to create of having only innocent fun when he asked Sam if he had Kathy Doyle's address on file.

Sam Barca growled, "I do not. I have enough trouble keeping track of folk who work for *this* paper. Still, I think she lives up on Telegraph Hill. If she has her own Bell telephone, she might be in their directory. Why do you ask?"

Stringer got back to his feet. "I owe the lady an apology, for openers," he explained. "If she's not shacked up with a sailor, she may let me make it up to her with a seafood dinner over on North Beach."

Sam Barca grinned knowingly. "That'd be about the

right distance between Fisherman's Wharf and her place on nearby Telegraph Hill, if you order some dago red to go with all those oysters, you sly dog."

Stringer grinned back sheepishly. "Don't talk dirty about fellow newspaper folk, Sam."

So Sam Barca said he was sorry as hell and asked, "If you're not as fond of redwoods as me, what did you have in mind for the coming weekend? Mayhaps collaborating on the Great American Novel?"

Stringer laughed. "I may have told you not to talk dirty, Sam," he said as he headed for the door, "but I sure as hell never told you to talk just plain silly!"

The hard-hitting, gun-slinging Pride of the Pinkertons is riding solo in this new action-packed series.

J.D. HARDIN'S
RAIDER

Sharpshooting Pinkertons Doc and Raider are legends in their own time, taking care of outlaws that the local sheriffs can't handle. Doc has decided to settle down and now Raider takes on the nastiest vermin the Old West has to offer single-handedly...charming the ladies along the way

__0-425-10757-4	**TIMBER WAR #10**	$2.75
__0-425-10851-1	**SILVER CITY AMBUSH #11**	$2.75
__0-425-10890-2	**THE NORTHWEST RAILROAD WAR #12**	$2.95
__0-425-10936-4	**THE MADMAN'S BLADE #13**	$2.95
__0-425-10985-2	**WOLF CREEK FEUD #14**	$2.95